FLEET WEDDING

In the gambling-mad salons of mid-18th century London no one is much surprised when the elegant Earl of Astbury wins Elyssa Fontwell during a game of cards. The Earl is horrified at winning plain, ailing Elyssa, and he immediately dispatches her to the country in the hope the damp will make a speedy end of her. However, Elyssa grows stronger and, stung by Lord Astbury's rejections of her, responds to Sir Courteney Hartington's flirting, unaware that he has sinister designs on her.

Books by Rachelle Edwards
in the Linford Romance Library:

WAGER FOR LOVE
DANGEROUS DANDY
THE SMITHFIELD BARGAIN
THE MARRIAGE BARGAIN
LORD HEATHBURY'S REVENGE

RACHELLE EDWARDS

FLEET WEDDING

Complete and Unabridged

LINFORD
Leicester

First published in Great Britain in 1981 by
Robert Hale Limited
London

First Linford Edition
published December 1995
by arrangement with
Robert Hale Limited
London

British Library CIP Data

Edwards, Rachelle
    Fleet wedding.—Large print ed.—
    Linford romance library
    I. Title II. Series
    823.914 [F]

    ISBN 0–7089–7790–1

Published by
F. A. Thorpe (Publishing) Ltd.
Anstey, Leicestershire
Set by Words & Graphics Ltd.
Anstey, Leicestershire
Printed and bound in Great Britain by
T. J. Press (Padstow) Ltd., Padstow, Cornwall

This book is printed on acid-free paper

1

THE evening was well-advanced. Candles burned low in their sockets and were replaced by a legion of servants at regular intervals.

A continual buzz of conversation in the room was punctuated at frequent intervals by bursts of laughter. The strains of harpsichord music now and again intruded as a young girl, hopeful of gaining the attention of a favoured gentleman, plucked at the chords. The air was heavy with the mingling perfumes of the orient, patchouli and musk.

At the card tables a number of people pursued their passion for gambling with careless abandon. Sir Rupert Fontwell, seated at one of the tables, licked his lips apprehensively, his pudgy fingers caressed the cards and he eyed his opponent with the unease of a habitual loser. At intervals he removed his gold pocket watch, peered at it anxiously before putting it away again, something noted with irony by his partner.

Around him in Lord Rivington's elegant drawing room many others were seated at card tables and a like number witnessing the play which was often reckless and almost always for enormous stakes. Those who eschewed the gaming, conversed in small groups, exchanging stories of the latest gossip and scandals in the *haute monde* of mid-eighteenth century London.

Many of the ladies, however, were gathered around the table where Sir Rupert was at play, for his opponent was the elegant Earl of Astbury, who held, for most females, a great fascination.

A bachelor and in his thirties, he was considered to possess a handsome countenance, with dark eyes which could either beguile or dismiss coldly with equal expertize, but despite his straightened circumstances he was considered to be a fair catch for those still unmarried. As a rake and a libertine he held an even greater attraction for the married ladies.

Sir Rupert continued to eye him uneasily as he reached for another card. By comparison the earl appeared to be perfectly relaxed. Dressed as always in the height of fashion — his brocade coat and velvet breeches were of the finest stuff — he was, however, not a dandy. Nothing of the extreme touched his sartorial elegance, although his French lawn shirt with its Flanders lace was the envy of many.

As the card game progressed more interest was directed towards the two, for they were known as deep gamblers and the stakes grew ever greater.

"I see that Astbury is all set to clear Fontwell of his funds," one matron confided in her companion, not without a certain amount of glee.

"That is not out of the ordinary," the other lady replied. "Astbury has been consistent in repairing the family fortunes by gaming since he came into the title, but Fontwell is so often the loser. I only wonder he has anything left to wager."

The other lady nodded sagely. "'Tis said his parlour is permanently occupied by duns."

"Fontwell always did play deep, but rarely with any degree of style. Now, Astbury is quite different. *He* invariably has Dame Fortune at his side of late."

The other lady laughed. "The reason for that is obvious, my dear; Dame Fortune is merely another female besotted by him. Oh, let us not pretend; Astbury is all charm and condescension. There is not one of us who does not linger in the hope of a word from his lips. Such style, such grace, is quite out of the common. Only see the French lawn and Flanders lace he wears! I am quite out of countenance for it is almost impossible to come by and horrendously expensive when one does."

Perspiration broke out on Sir Rupert's

brow and he mopped it with a lace-edged handkerchief. As he did so Lord Astbury, who seemed still at ease despite the stakes, took the opportunity to look around him. He bestowed a charming smile on several ladies who were watching him, much to their delight and consternation, and then, as he was about to return his attention to the cards, he caught the eye of a delightful creature who had been attempting to flirt with him throughout the evening.

Despite his involvement in the game his gaze was bound to linger. She was sitting on a sofa next to someone he recognized as Lady Fontwell and he knew she had rarely left that lady's side throughout the evening. The lovely creature lowered her eyes when Lord Astbury glanced at her, and then hid her face behind her fan. The gesture did not dismay him, however. He was far too experienced in the ways of women to mistake the signs of encouragement for anything else, and suddenly he was anxious to be finished with the cards, in order to engage in quite another sort of game.

Sir Rupert cleared his throat and Lord Astbury gave him his attention once again. "You seem a trifle out of countenance, Sir Rupert," the earl observed. "Perchance you would like to call it quits at this stage and cut your losses."

"No, no. Pray let us continue. 'Tis only the heat in here which has discomposed me."

The earl looked to a gentleman who was standing nearby and said, "Mr Grabney, if you please."

Accordingly, the gentleman handed Sir Rupert his silk fan which the baronet opened with alacrity and began to swish to and fro with a great deal of fervour as his opponent began to deal the cards. As the game progressed Sir Rupert became more and more agitated. A large amount of money piled up on the table and yet Lord Astbury still displayed not the slightest unease.

At last, as the game neared its end, he turned the final card. A few observers gasped. The ladies looked unashamedly delighted and Lord Astbury sat back in the chair.

Sir Rupert, despite being a consistent loser managed to look rather taken aback before saying in a mock-jocular fashion, "Well, all is now yours, Astbury, and I confess," he laughed gruffly, "my pockets are to let."

"Then that, I regret, must be the end of our game," the earl replied as he gathered together the money and vouchers piled before him.

Once again Sir Rupert mopped his brow. Lord Astbury, as he put away his considerable winnings suddenly became aware that the delightful creature he had been admiring all evening was now approaching their table and he sat back once again in order to admire her.

Her dark eyes, as they raked over him seemed to flash with fire, her ample bosom strained at the stays of her Genoa velvet gown in a most pleasing way. Her entire manner promised ecstasy.

Sir Rupert said gruffly. "Ah, Sophia, my dear, if only you had been by my side Dame Fortune might have looked more kindly upon me."

The girl was immediately downcast. "I am so sorry, Papa. If only I had known . . ."

Again the flirtatious look in the earl's direction despite her apparent sorrow. His blood quickened in his veins. She wore patches at the corners of her eyes and one near her lips. She was, he thought, one of the sauciest baggages he had ever encountered in polite society.

Nearby someone began to play the harpsichord and he glanced over his shoulder, irritated that anyone should divert his attention from the gorgeous Sophia and the triumph of his sizeable win.

Seated at the instrument was a girl of a similar age to the delectable Sophia, but this one could not hold his interest as she had done. She was thin and pale, and her playing of French songs was interrupted from time to time by bouts of coughing. Lord Astbury gave her a pitying glance, for it was obvious she was not long for this world.

Returning his attention to Sophia, he subjected her to one of his most charming smiles and was gratified to see the colour rise to her cheeks.

Then he looked at the discomforted baronet. "It has been a most enjoyable evening," he conceded.

"For you, I do not doubt, and let me remind you, my lord, it is not yet ended. You must certainly allow me the opportunity of winning back a little of my money."

The earl's eyes narrowed. "Indeed, I shall, when you have the means to provide a stake in a further game."

To no one's surprise Sir Rupert looked even more discomforted. He glanced around uneasily. "Perchance Lord Rivington will be so good as to afford us the use of his cabinet where we can discuss the matter in more privacy than is afforded us here."

The Marquis of Rivington came hurrying up to them, a cloud of musk perfume wafting along with him. "Certainly, certainly; be pleased to come this way, gentlemen."

Lord Astbury got to his feet slowly, unfurling himself to full height. He looked a mite suspicious, for he was aware Sir Rupert had been known to resort to dubious means to fund his passion for gaming. Sophia appeared to be vexed at not gaining his full attention and moved away. The earl cast her a regretful glance and made to follow the two other men.

As he crossed the room he beckoned to a friend, Captain of Dragoons Freddie Wyatt who had been engrossed in his own game of hazard.

"What's amiss?" the captain immediately asked on seeing the dark expression on his friend's face.

"I am not quite certain. I suspect that Sir Rupert is attempting to raise a further stake in the hope of winning back all he has lost tonight."

"Oh, the fellow is always out of funds. He can only provide a promissory note which will merely make you another dun outside his door. Take your winnings and be satisfied."

"Let us at least hear his proposition, Freddie. Judging from what I know of him I have just won everything he possesses at this moment, but you may be quite certain I shall accept no further vouchers from him this night."

Captain Wyatt cast his friend a sharp look as the drawing room door was flung open by two footmen and they stepped into a small ante-room.

★ ★ ★

Myles Alaric Aloysious Trent, eighth Earl of Astbury had been born only on the fringe of the aristocracy with no thought to the elevated situation he would one day inherit. His schoolday friends called him Foxy, mainly because of his astute brain and skill with cards. Now he had come into the title quite unexpectedly and his elevation was not entirely welcome.

The seventh earl had been no more than a distant relative, a childless widower who had spent the most part of his life dissipating his fortune. The young Myles Trent had not set eyes upon his relative above two or three times in his life and had settled down to a career in the third King's Own Dragoon Guards when news of his relative's death had reached him.

As well as the title, he had inherited countless debts which he had succeeded in paying off gradually, mainly through his success at cards. Astute as ever, the earl knew such good fortune could not last and his friends urged him to marry an heiress to give him the means he needed to maintain his position. Although the notion found favour with Lord Astbury in principle, nevertheless he had not so far found a well-endowed female who was also to his taste, although this was something his acquaintances considered an impossibility anyway.

"Look favourably upon a portion," Captain Wyatt had once told him, "and then you may have the means to look lasciviously at someone else's wife."

"I would wish to have a choice of both," the earl had replied.

Now he strode across the room to where Sir Rupert was seated by Lord Rivington's desk.

"A glass of claret?" their host asked.

"If you please," the earl answered, fixing Sir Rupert with a fierce stare. As Lord Rivington handed them each a glass he asked, "Now what is all this about, Fontwell? I understood your pockets are to let."

Sir Rupert still looked flushed. "Yes, indeed, Astbury. I shall not mince my words; your win has put me in dun territory."

Lord Astbury was, of course, unsurprised, but yet he stiffened, saying,

"I trust you are able to honour the vouchers already in my possession."

The other man laughed although a mite uncomfortably. "Indeed yes, but I must ask in all humility for a chance to redeem a little of what I have lost tonight."

"At any time, Fontwell," he replied drinking the claret. "As soon as you have the means, in fact."

He walked across the room and stood near the fireplace, looking up at a portrait of one of Lord Rivington's ancestors. Sir Rupert continued to look discomforted as he toyed with his handkerchief. During his nervous fidgeting his wig had been knocked askew whereas the earl looked as though he had only just stepped out of his dressing room.

"I do — now," came the breathless answer, "if you are agreeable."

Turning around, Lord Astbury put down the empty glass and waved away a refill. He came across the room once again and sat down on the edge of a table, fixing the baronet with his dark eyed stare.

"You truly surprise me, Sir Rupert."

The other man smiled faintly. The Earl drew out his snuff box and took a pinch. After he had put the box away he brushed his breeches with his handkerchief. All the time Sir Rupert eyed him uneasily.

"You are a sporting man, Lord Astbury," he ventured at last. "I am persuaded you, more than most men, will appreciate the wager I am about to propose. It is something of the greatest value to me," he added.

The earl's eyebrows rose a fraction. Captain Wyatt shrugged slightly, but looked most interested.

"If you have some ruined mansion in the depths of the country, I am not much interested," the earl told him with a languid wave of his hand, "for I have one of my own."

Sir Rupert laughed harshly. "No, indeed. 'Tis something of far more value than mere property."

"A diamond?" Captain Wyatt asked. "A ruby, perchance?"

"Nothing so mundane, Captain Wyatt. No jewel could be as valuable as what I am about to offer."

"Speak out then, man," the earl urged, becoming interested at last, "but recall I am aware you have no property of worth any more."

"I have something which may be worth a great deal to you. If you are willing, you may play for the hand of my dear, dear daughter."

There was a few seconds' silence in the room although the conversation and laughter in the adjoining room filtered through to them.

"You jest!" It was Captain Wyatt who spoke at last. "That is an outrageous suggestion. Your daughter indeed!"

"Can you think of anything I possess which is of greater value?"

"Your *daughter*," the earl repeated and then he began to laugh out loud. "You truly make a good jest and I am vastly amused, I own."

Sir Rupert's eyes bulged. "Gad, sir, I do not jest."

The earl's laughter died away abruptly. "No, indeed you do not, but, sir, what should I do with a gentleman's daughter if I won her?"

"Wed her, my lord. You need a wife, do you not? She's a fine, comely girl. A good help to her mother, let me tell you. Your houses will be run with the maximum efficiency and economy."

"They are now."

"She is infinitely accomplished, and educated by a French governess. My dear, Astbury, you really do need a wife. Every man should enjoy such bliss, and a chit such as she is worth more than pure gold, but if it is gold you desire let me tell you that my daughter has her own." He paused, knowing he had gained the earl's attention at last. "Oh, indeed. Her maternal grandfather left her a modest fortune of two thousand pounds a year, which alas I am unable to touch and which can only begin to be paid on her marriage."

The earl had at first been stunned by the proposition but once the shock began to wear off he recalled that more outrageous wagers had been made. His mind returned to the gorgeous Sophia who was, it seemed an heiress, too. He could do a great deal worse and for a man in his situation marriage would not be a bind.

"You cannot possibly put up your daughter as a wager," Captain Wyatt protested, laughing in bewilderment.

"There is no law to say I cannot," came the reply, but all the time Sir Rupert was watching the earl.

Lord Astbury got to his feet and stood up straight, taller than any of the men in the room. "Very well, Sir Rupert, if that is your wish. I shall give you the opportunity to redeem your property, but if you lose, your daughter becomes my wife."

"A wise decision, my lord, although I was in no doubt of it."

Captain Wyatt came across the room and, catching his friend by the arm, he swung him around. "Foxy, do you know what you are about?"

The earl cast him a bland look. "It seems obvious enough to me, Freddie, and do be good enough to unhand me. This coat cost me dear and I have no mind to see it wrinkled."

Obligingly Captain Wyatt let him go, saying angrily, "This evening is like to cost you even more dear."

"Don't be so Friday-faced," the earl chided and his friend retorted darkly, "Do not expect my sympathy when you fry in your own grease."

"Are you not a gambling man, Captain Wyatt?" Sir Rupert asked in a conversational tone.

"Not above the ordinary, sir."

"Then you cannot presume to lecture Lord Astbury. Only he knows the exhilaration of risking all on the turn of a card in the hope of winning a great prize."

"In most cases, if I may say so, sir, the 'prize' is not like to object."

Sir Rupert laughed gruffly. "I assure

you, my dear fellow, this daughter of mine is most obedient."

"You risk a great deal this night," Lord Rivington was forced to point out.

"Lord Astbury and I recognize it very well, my lord."

Sir Rupert got to his feet, quickly took off his coat and, turning it inside out, put it back on again.

"Dame Fortune will not be at your side on this occasion, Astbury."

The earl smiled and made a slight bow. "She might just decide to favour your daughter, sir."

2

N O one looked at them amiss as they came back into the drawing room. Lord Astbury glanced around until he caught sight of Sophia who was now sitting near to the girl who had been playing the harpsichord. The panniers of Sophia's fashionable gown took up almost all of the sofa, and the other girl was obliged to sit right at the end. Sophia cast him a smile and he determined to play as never before to win her hand. The other girl was intent upon her embroidery except for when she was forced by a bout of coughing to stop and resort to her vinaigrette.

The two players returned to their previous seats and when it was noticed that Sir Rupert had reversed his coat it became apparent stakes were now very high indeed and a crowd gathered.

Within minutes the nature of the wager was known and a wave of excitement swept the room.

"This goes beyond anything I have ever witnessed," Lady Rivington remarked to her husband.

"Camdon wagered his four matched greys a month or two ago," was the reply. "He was exceeding fond of them."

"Of all people to agree to it, though, I would have not considered Astbury to be one of them."

"The Fontwell chit is an heiress in her own right."

"Ah . . . " Lady Rivington answered knowingly and went to watch the game,

As the cards were being shuffled by a third person the earl caught sight of Sophia in the crowd. Her eyes were bright with excitement and with some considerable difficulty he drew his attention away from her and to the cards.

Sir Rupert licked his lips as the pack was placed in the centre of the baize.

"A simple draw, Astbury?"

"As you wish."

The earl himself had become afflicted uncharacteristically by tension although it was true to say he had never played for such high stakes before.

The baronet cut the pack and then leaned forward. His hand lingered on the pack for what seemed to be an endless time during which the earl watched him, a smile playing about the corners of his lips. Then, almost abruptly, Sir Rupert drew a card towards him. Almost fearfully he gazed at it and then he began to smile before revealing it to all those craning their necks to see. The Queen of Diamonds. A murmur of excitement rippled around the room. It was an excellent card and only an extreme of good fortune could win the wager for Lord Astbury, who was now likely to lose all he had gained during the evening's gaming.

When he shifted slightly in his seat the murmuring died away leaving practically no sound in the room save a good deal of heavy breathing and the swishing of fans.

"Go on, Foxy," urged Captain Wyatt who was standing at his side. "Draw a card and let us have an end to it."

"This is a moment to savour," came the nonchalant reply.

However he did then lean forward to draw a card from the top of the pack. Sir Rupert's eyes almost popped out of his head and somewhere in the room the thin girl started to cough, a sound which at that tense moment cut him to the quick.

After several seconds he, too, looked at the card before drawing a small sigh.

"How appropriate," he murmured, turning it uppermost for all to see. "The King of Hearts."

Everyone began to talk at once. Triumphantly the earl got to his feet as a host of acquaintances hurried to congratulate him.

"A fair win," Sir Rupert conceded

with a sigh, although he looked not a mite put out.

"Shall we adjourn?" the earl suggested, unable to see Sophia now for the crowds which milled around him.

"Congratulations, my lord," a sarcastic voice drawled in his ear and when he turned, the man added, "Lieutenant Desmond Fontwell, my lord. You've just won m'sister and you are most welcome to her."

The lieutenant had the same florid complexion as his father and his tendency to plumpness, too. The earl could not imagine from whom Sophia inherited her looks, for Lady Fontwell was as plain as a pipe stem.

"I thank you," the earl replied, not liking the man's attitude, nor his reminder that the girl had been won in a game of chance.

"Have my wife and daughter sent in," Sir Rupert called out as he crossed the room.

"Do you realize what you've done?" Captain Wyatt asked in a harsh whisper.

"You've won a wife, by gad!"

The earl grinned. "Is it not you who's forever plaguing me to take a wife?"

"A daughter of Sir Rupert Fontwell, though. I cannot conceive she will be anything but trouble."

The earl seemed not the least put out. He accepted the congratulations of his acquaintances with alacrity.

"Come, Freddie, let us go and be acquainted with the bride."

He excused himself from those who milled about him and the ante-room was a haven of peace by comparison. When the lackey closed the door, most of the excited chatter was shut out.

Lord Rivington was again pouring claret and Sir Rupert was once more flushed, this time with pleasure.

As he returned his coat to its proper side he said, "You are a most fortunate man. My daughter is both abstemious and modest."

The earl accepted another glass of wine and did not reply, for he regarded

Sir Rupert as blind to his daughter's true nature, although that was irrelevant now. Sophia Fontwell was no milk and water miss; she was a hot-blooded female who would suit him well. If she lived up to the promise in her smile he would consider himself the most fortunate of men.

Sir Rupert raised his glass. "Your good health." He took a sip before adding, a mite regretfully, "I did not truly wish to lose her in such a way, gentlemen — you may be certain of that — but I always hoped for a high position for my daughter. 'Tis no more than she deserves."

"She will be well cared for," the earl assured him although it seemed this was not something which concerned the baronet overmuch. He was strutting about like a turkey cock. The earl had never seen a loser in such buoyant spirits. However, he appreciated that it was he who benefited the most.

"I do not propose to delay the wedding," he informed Sir Rupert, "for I see no advantage in doing so."

"Very wise. The sooner you are wed the better in view of the circumstances. Now, where is the chit?"

The door opened and Lady Fontwell edged into the room with some difficulty due to the width of her paniers. "Ah, Maria, where is Elyssa? Lord Astbury is awaiting her impatiently."

"She is recovering her composure," snapped his wife. "She was quite overcome which is no more than might be expected." She shot the earl a furious look. "Really, Fontwell, you should at least have given us some warning of what you intended to do."

Sir Rupert banged his glass down on the table. "Oh, cease your prattle. Your daughter is going to be a countess. Is that not what you have always wished for?"

"In such a manner! It's disgraceful." She glanced scathingly at the earl again before adding, "He's a worse scapegrace than you are, which is to say a great deal."

"I am sorry you feel that way, ma'am," the earl answered, bowing low. "I shall earnestly endeavour to make you look upon me more favourably in the time to come."

His charm was so effusive that Lady Fontwell was a mite taken aback and then she said grudgingly, "I shall await that time eagerly," and then proceeded to ease her bulky skirts into a chair. When she had done so she proceeded to fan herself furiously.

"You must forgive Lady Fontwell her attitude," her husband begged.

The earl accepted another glass of claret from their host and Captain Wyatt replied, "Sir Rupert, we are all taken aback somewhat by the outcome of this evening's events."

By this time the earl had partaken of several glasses of claret but suddenly, despite the pleasant haze which deemed to have formed around him, something did occur to him and he turned to his future father-in-law.

"Fontwell, did I not hear you call

your daughter Elyssa?"

The baronet was also full of good cheer. "Naturally, for that is her name. Fetching is it not? Elyssa Carlotta Marguerite. I chose the names myself when she was born."

The earl put one hand to his head which was not at all clear. "I am becoming a mite confused, but I am persuaded she was named Sophia. You did call her Sophia."

Sir Rupert's smile faded and he put his glass down on the table. "*Sophia?*" He laughed gruffly. "No, bless you. Sophia is my son's wife." He smiled again. "She has always called me Papa, but I have only the one daughter."

The earl looked as if he had been struck by a thunderbolt. Almost under his breath he said, "Sophia is not your daughter."

"No, by jove, she is not!" Sir Rupert answered, roaring with laughter.

The earl's eyes opened wide. "Then who in damnation is Elyssa?"

"Ah, here she is!" her proud father

cried, smiling happily once again. "Elyssa, my dear, do come in. You have been keeping your bridegroom waiting which does not augur well."

The earl turned on his heel to see his future wife enter the room, slowly and fearfully. It was with total disbelief that he stared at the thin, pale creature with weak lungs for whom pity had briefly touched his heart.

He may have been horrified at his own error, but the girl looked totally bemused by the turn of events. Not only was she pale but her eyes were rimmed with red, indicating the shedding of tears not too long before.

She glanced around the room, her eyes studiously avoiding a hard look at any of them. Coughing a little she sank into a curtsey.

"Lord Astbury cannot wait to make you his wife," her father informed her gleefully.

"You go too fast," he said quickly and Sir Rupert turned on his heel to look at him in astonishment. "I have

31

been in error," he went on in a whisper, putting down his glass. "This was not whom I expected when the wager was made."

Sir Rupert came hurrying across the room. "You agreed to wed my daughter, my lord, and I have only the one."

Uncharacteristically confused the earl turned away, unable to bear gazing upon so pathetic a creature who looked frightened out of her wits.

"You cannot expect to go further with this, Sir Rupert. Let us call it quits now. We are all too bosky to know what we are about."

"We are all quite sober!" he protested. "Or at least we were when the wager was agreed upon." On receiving no answer from the earl he demanded, "Do you mean to renegade on a wager, Lord Astbury? A man of honour such as yourself. I cannot believe it possible."

The earl smiled weakly. "I accepted only to enable you to chance your luck again."

"How noble of you, but had I won I would have taken my winnings with alacrity, and I would consider myself dishonoured if you did not do so, too."

"But, Sir Rupert," the earl went on desperately, "only think; the stake was your daughter. I would not for anything take her as payment for a gambling debt."

"You were anxious enough when you thought your prize was Sophia. Let me tell you she would lead you a merry jig as she does my son. She spends his every last halfpenny and cuckolds him at every turn. Elyssa is worth ten of Sophia."

"I do not doubt it, Sir Rupert," the earl replied in a weary tone, wondering how to wriggle out of the situation if the baronet was in no mind to let him.

"And yet you insult my child."

"I beg your pardon, sir, but you must see it won't do."

"No, by jove, it will not. You shall

meet me over this Astbury."

The earl turned to look at him in astonishment. Captain Wyatt said, eyeing the baronet's portly and puffing frame, "Lord Astbury is a superlative swordsman, sir."

The girl in question, although she could not hear what it was they argued about was well-aware of the dissension and after a moment or two ran to her mother and dissolved into tears, something which did not endear her further to her husband-to-be.

Taking advantage of the diversion Sir Rupert took the earl to one side, saying, "This matter can easily be resolved, I feel, without resorting to extreme measures."

"You relieve me, Fontwell; be pleased to explain how."

"Take pity on her, my lord, for she is not like to live long, and it is her mother's dearest wish to see her wed. No other consideration would have prompted me to act as I have done today. And recall," he added slyly, "she is not without means. Whatever becomes of Elyssa, her fortune will remain in the hands of the man she marries."

Sir Rupert stood back the better to view the result of his words. Lord Astbury glanced at the girl who was being comforted by her mother.

At length he said, "You're a coxcombe, Fontwell."

"It takes one to recognize another, my lord."

"I'll wed the chit. As an honourable man who has no wish to run through so unequal a match, I shall honour the wager, but do not suppose I shall do more, sir. The error was mine and I must bear the consequences, but never again shall I flirt with Dame Fortune."

"I cannot credit that, Astbury. Gaming is deep in your blood as it is in mine." He turned on his heel, saying, "All is well; the final arrangements have been made. Lord Astbury is pleased to marry you, my dear."

The girl looked up in alarm and Sir

Rupert went on, addressing Captain Wyatt, "No doubt you will be groomsman, sir."

Startled, the captain replied, "If his lordship condescends to ask me."

The earl started across the room. "Make whatever arrangements you will, Fontwell, and then inform me."

"Why delay at all? There is no cause. Why not seal the knot immediately?" he suggested, causing the earl to turn on his heel again.

"At this hour?"

"The Mayfair Chapel is open all hours. I am persuaded Lord Rivington would be good enough to send one of his lackeys to alert the clergyman to be ready for our arrival."

"Have you no concern for our daughter's sensibilities?" his wife asked.

"My dear, that is precisely why I propose no delay. Only imagine the effect prattle will have upon us all. A *fait accompli* is the only remedy."

The earl was angry. "So you propose a Fleet wedding eh? Well, I own it is fitting. Why not use the Fleet Chapel itself?"

"The Mayfair is far more genteel," Sir Rupert decided, ignoring the earl's sarcasm. "My Lord Rivington, if you please."

The marquis departed to instruct one of his servants and the baronet added, glancing around the room, "We are all splendidly attired for a wedding. You, my lord, have on your silver waistcoat. It couldn't be more fitting."

Ignoring his jollity the earl turned his angry gaze upon the girl. "Have you nothing to say, miss?"

Elyssa Fontwell cowered in her mother's arms. "No, my lord."

Sir Rupert laughed. "See, Astbury, she has the making of a perfect wife. What man could desire more?"

The earl shot him a look of disgust and then the girl ventured, her eyes wide, "Perchance, we should take a little time to ponder on the wisdom of this matter."

Her father shot her a furious look.

"Be silent, wench, and do not speak unless addressed."

Her cheeks grew rather red and the earl felt a stirring of pity. So far no one had considered her feelings in the matter and it was altogether possible she experienced as much disgust as he, although he doubted if that could be so.

Lord Rivington returned, nibbing his hands together. It had been for him, as the host, a most satisfying evening. No card party had ended so sensationally since Lord Kingsby and Mr Thurloe had accused each other of cheating.

"A footman has departed to wake the clergyman, and your carriages are outside the door. You may leave with no further delay if that is what you wish."

"To your wedding," Sir Rupert cried, urging his wife and daughter towards the door.

Elyssa Fontwell cast the earl a reproachful look before doing as she was bid.

Lord Astbury watched them go, his face dark with anger and then he strode out of the room followed closely by Captain Wyatt.

"To my wedding, Freddie. I can scarcely conceive this is happening."

"You were eager enough a while ago," his friend pointed out.

"Ah yes, but now I'd as lief be going to the devil!"

3

DESPITE the lateness of the hour the London streets were still awash with activity. Link men lighted pedestrians and carriages through the dark streets whilst sedan chairmen weaved between them bearing their heavy loads. Footpads and cutpurses lurked in the numerous dark alleys, awaiting those foolhardy enough to venture past alone.

Lord Astbury leaned his head against the squabs of the splendid carriage he had recently acquired.

"I am fit only for Bedlam, Freddie. I must have been foxed to accept such a wager."

"You hold your liquor so well it is always difficult to tell. Had I thought you were foxed I would have stopped you accepting the wager."

"It makes no matter. I always knew

the day would arrive when I played one hand too many."

Captain Wyatt looked at him. "We are talking as if you are ruined! I know the chit is not to your taste — she cannot be to anyone's taste! — but recall you are considerably richer than you were a few hours ago."

"Can you imagine, though, being wed to Elyssa Fontwell?"

"As much as it will make any difference to you, Foxy. Marriage changes nothing save a man's fortune. Lord, think how many men are wed to plain, ineffectual females for reasons of family and fortune."

"I never had a taste for that and cannot see myself living with her in connubial bliss."

The young man laughed. "Ever since our schooldays you've enjoyed the company of fetching chits and marriage to any kind of female is not like to change that, my friend."

"What of the girl, though? She looked

as if she was about to be clapped in Newgate."

Captain Wyatt sighed. "She ought to be glad to be away from that father of hers. Foxy, if I didn't know better I'd have thought he connived at this. He was mightily pleased to be rid of her."

"Wouldn't you in his place?" the earl asked, his voice filled with irony. "Even with her portion she hasn't attracted any serious suitors."

"The reason is obvious," his friend mused. "The poor creature's days are numbered. Who wishes to wed a chit who's like to be dead in a six month?"

"Someone who does not want her for a wife," the earl replied, his voice heavy with irony, adding a mite cruelly, "Let us hope that the next six months pass quickly and that they are uncommonly *damp*. Ah, here we are!"

The carriage drew to a halt behind another which was already outside the chapel, a place that had become notorious for its solemnizing of runaway marriages.

The earl peered at it as he climbed down from the carriage. "The place looks the more suited to funerals than weddings."

Sir Rupert and Lady Fontwell were already inside with their daughter. The chapel had been hastily lighted with the minimum number of candles necessary, which added to the funereal appearance of the place. From the expressions on their faces it was obvious they suspected the bridegroom would not, after all, attend. The baronet looked immediately relieved, but it was difficult to discern what their daughter felt for she turned away the moment the earl and his friend entered the chapel.

The clergyman, who had been summoned from his bed, was wearing his dressing gown and was hard-pressed to stop yawning. With his frizzed wig hastily donned and not quite straight he anxiously urged them forward.

"The hour grows late, my lords," he ventured.

"This is not how I saw myself

surrendering my bachelor status," the earl confided in his friend as they continued to hesitate at the back of the chapel.

"Nor, I dare say, are you the kind of man with whom she expected to end her maidenly situation."

The earl looked at him askance. "My dear fellow, what can you think of me? Such a poor specimen of womanhood is like to expire if a gentleman so much as smiles in her direction. For her health's sake I must keep my distance but that will be no sacrifice. She will have white flowers at her funeral."

The young man looked surprised. "I had no notion you were so callous, Foxy."

"Callous?" his friend retorted. "I do her a kindness."

Captain Wyatt laughed loudly then and Sir Rupert called, "My Lord Astbury, if you are ready; Reverend Fairfield awaits."

The two friends went to join the others. "Sir Rupert," the earl chided, his voice heavy with irony, "I appreciate Reverend Fairfield's haste to be done with us, but marriage is not something into which a man should rush."

The humour of the remark bypassed the baronet, but the earl was certain the girl stifled a laugh behind her hand which surprised him somewhat.

Still trying not to yawn Reverend Fairfield began to recite the wedding service in a dull voice devoid of all emotion. It took but a few minutes without the normal ceremonial and when the couple were pronounced man and wife there followed an expectant pause. The earl then turned to his bride to whom he stiffly bowed before striding quickly out of the chapel and into the street.

Before anyone had a chance to realize he had actually gone, the sound of wheels and horses hooves could be heard on the cobblestones outside as the carriage moved away.

* * *

His head ached abominably as the sedan chair stopped outside the house in Bedford Square, so much so that the chairmen had to help the earl out of the conveyance and up the steps where a footman opened the door and relieved them of their burden.

The evening which had started so well and turned so disastrous, had ended not too badly after all. The earl had drunk himself senseless in the arms of one of his favourite doxies who resided in a certain establishment not too far from Covent Garden.

The chairmen were rewarded well for their assistance. In his newfound affluence the earl could well afford it, but even in more straightened times he was well-known for his open-handed generosity.

The town house in Bedford Square was one he had inherited with the title, only then it had been badly run down with peeling plasterwork and little furniture of value. Now, newly renovated, the earl was proud of all he had achieved. Newly-fashionable mahogany furniture was to be found in every room and an army of liveried servants kept it in good order.

It was the house-steward himself who took his master's hat, cane and gloves as he entered the hall, none too steadily; something the servants were accustomed to seeing.

"I trust your lordship has had a convivial evening?" the man commented as he slotted Lord Astbury's ebony stick into the stand which held the others in his collection.

"It was most uncommon," the earl admitted, drawing a deep breath.

Suddenly he became aware of others present in the cavernous hall. He turned abruptly on his heel, glaring across the gloom. Seated in a murky corner, accompanied by her maid and surrounded by a number of cloakbags and bandboxes was none other than the new countess.

She was sitting, eyes downcast, still wearing a cloak and a chipstraw hat.

"Hell and damnation!" he swore, oblivious now to his aching head and his unsteady limbs.

Forgetfulness, it now appeared, was strictly a temporary matter.

"The young lady arrived some hours ago, my lord, announcing she was Lady Astbury. As I know the late earl was a widower of many years standing I thought to summon the custodians of Bedlam, but she was insistent and seemed rational enough. She is obviously a lady of quality, my lord."

"It is I who should be in Bedlam, Fothergill. This lady is indeed the Countess of Astbury and my wife."

The lackey looked taken aback. "My lord, I beg your pardon . . . "

The earl waved his hand in the air. "There is no cause to apologize, Fothergill. When I left here this evening I was still a bachelor."

With no further ado he strode up to his wife, towering over her for some moments before she raised her eyes

48

which he noted were filled with the most utter misery. Once again his anger could not be sustained and in place of it he could feel only pity.

"Papa insisted that I come," she said in a whisper. "I am so very sorry; there was nought I could do."

Suddenly aware that several young housemaids, abroad early to clean and set the fires, were watching and listening avidly he waved his hand at them angrily.

"Have you nothing better to do?"

Fearful of his anger they scurried away and he looked to his house steward again. "Fothergill, see that Lady Astbury is shown upstairs."

The servant's face remained inscrutable as if such odd events occurred regularly. "Which room, my lord?"

"Mine, of course, you fool."

The girl gave him a grateful look and with her maid started to follow the servant up the stairs. The earl stayed at the foot of the stairs until she was out of sight before striding into his library and slamming the door behind him with unusual force.

A few seconds later a housemaid — with coal tongs still clutched in her hand came scurrying out of the room, rushing back to the kitchen to impart the exciting news to all those who had not been privileged to overhear for themselves.

4

IT was approaching noon when a certain Mr Charles Lamont climbed the stairs to his mother's boudoir in a house in Soho Square. When he entered he found her reclining on a day bed, feeding marchpane to her pet monkey who at the interruption began to bound about the room in agitation.

"Charles, dearest, how nice it is to see you, and so early in the day, too!"

She held out her arms and he went to give her a dutiful kiss. Kitty Lamont had been quite a beauty in her day and was still considered to be a handsome woman. Her son, however, with his slight build and pale colouring no amount of powder could disguise, inherited some of the weaker traits of his late father.

Mrs Lamont patted the end of the sofa. "Now come and sit by me and tell me all your *on dits*."

"There is but one of any import."

"Then do not delay in imparting it to me."

"The news is terrible," he gasped, unable to control himself any longer as he stooped and weaved in an effort to avoid the monkey which had a disconcerting habit of pouncing on him from the chandelier.

"Are we at war?" his mother asked, chewing on a piece of marchpane with a nonchalance which irritated her already agitated son.

"Would that we were. No, it is far worse. I have just left the Cocoa Tree and all the tattle is of Astbury."

"Oh, I might have known."

"He has taken a wife!"

"Is that all?"

"All! Wives have children and children inherit titles, Mamma."

"You surely didn't expect him to remain a bachelor all his life. And recall, you are a very distant relative, Charles. It was a faint hope."

"Astbury was only distantly related to the late earl and he inherited."

"A mountain of debts."

"Which he has discharged. Oh, dammit, Mamma, we are rich and I want that title."

"Even if he hadn't married, he's a young sprig and he might have outlived you."

"Not the way he lives, Mamma. If he doesn't die from drink, it'll be in a duel over some doxy, or worse," he added darkly.

His mother laughed. "Don't be so certain of that. Foxy can take all that and more."

"Our late unlamented Prince of Wales burned himself out and expired unexpectedly," he pointed out and then became annoyed again, "Really, Mamma, I expected at least you to sympathize. One could almost think you were besotted with him."

Mrs Lamont smiled dreamily. "Foxy

and I have had our moments."

Her son looked horrified and then said resentfully, "He won her in a wager at Rivington's last night."

Mrs Lamont finished the last piece of marchpane and carefully wiped her hands on a lace handkerchief.

"Yes, I know, and that hardly augurs well for wedded bliss. Heaven knows, marriage is difficult enough when contracted in the normal way."

"How do you know? I only discovered it myself an hour ago."

"Durkell called in earlier and I heard all about it from him. He was at Rivington House last night so I have the truth of it from him. What I would not have given to have been there myself." She glanced at her son. "La! Fontwell's chit is as sickly as they come. She's not going to bear him healthy sons to inherit the title, and if he is half the man I know him to be he won't even try. He'll be as mad as a weaver when he sobers up this morning."

The young man brightened a little. "He may even apply for an annulment."

"Do not depend upon that. Astbury is exceedingly proud, but have no fear, you will get that title yet, my dear."

Charles Lamont flicked some imaginary snuff from his pink brocade coat. "I trust that you are correct because I really do want to become the Earl of Astbury one day."

His mother eyed him curiously. "I never realized before now how important it is. As I said, the poor girl is as sickly as they come." She drew a sigh. "It won't be long before dear Foxy mourns the loss of his young bride. It would not surprise me over much if Fontwell only wished to see her wed to avoid the expense of a funeral." She paused for a moment before adding, "'Tis as well black becomes me so well, my dear."

Considerably cheered, her son got to his feet only to have the monkey snatch at his exquisitely powdered wig. The young man only just managed to push the creature away before it lifted the wig from his head. Thwarted it snapped at Charles who cried out in rage.

"Oh you bad, bad boy, Ninky," crooned Mrs Lamont.

Grimacing, her son wrapped his handkerchief around the wound saying, "I really cannot conceive why you keep that creature, Mamma."

She shrugged. "Because he amuses me and so few others do that." She looked suddenly thoughtful. "I wonder if Hartington has heard the news yet?"

"Sir Courtney Hartington?" her son asked. "What has he to do with it?"

"Nothing of any consequence, only his estate neighbours Astbury's and they dislike each other heartily. Hartington is such a dandy. Astbury cannot abide his perfume! But I declare Hartington will find this vastly amusing."

"No doubt he and his cronies will go dancing about in the moonlight to celebrate the wedding," Charles Lamont added dryly, something which made his mother laugh.

"Do not scorn such an activity, my dear boy; it can be vastly amusing."

He took her hand in his uninjured one and raised it to his lips. "I had best go with no further delay to Bedford Square and pay my respects to Lord Astbury."

His mother gave him a wry look. "I do hope that the words don't choke you, dearest."

"So do I," he answered from the door.

"And do not forget to put some court plaster on that bite."

"I shall do more than that; I shall call in Dr Jukes to bleed me as soon as this unpleasant errand is performed." His eyes narrowed with malice. "All the time I shall be hoping she gets caught in the rain and receive a fatal drenching."

"A draught of cold air will do as well."

Mrs Lamont's laughter could be heard as he hurried down the stairs, but a scowl remained on his face even when he hailed a sedan chair. He was not really comforted by what his mother had told him, for he knew very well sickly people often survived their healthy friends.

* * *

"What did the footman want?" Elyssa asked anxiously as her maid closed the door and came back into the room.

The maid cast her mistress a pitying look. "Lord Astbury requests the pleasure of your company in the library, ma'am."

"There'll be little enough pleasure in that. Oh, what is to become of us?"

"I couldn't say, ma'am, but no doubting it won't be as bad as you fear."

Elyssa sighed and seemed not at all comforted by her maid's words. Then she asked, "Do I look all right?" Before the maid could answer, she went on, "As if it matters. I have seen the way he looks upon me. He despises me and I cannot blame him. No man has paid more dearly for his drunken folly."

Distress and agitation caused her to begin coughing and the maid hurried to the dresser. "Let me give you some of your linctus, ma'am. It will soothe your lungs."

"Nothing will do that, I fear." But nevertheless she took the proffered spoonful.

The coughing did abate and Elyssa caught her breath again. Then she began to smooth down the skirt of her silk plush gown before hesitating to go to the door.

"What shall I say to him, Dora? How shall I face him? 'Twas difficult enough at night when the dark afforded us a mantle. I shall not be able to say anything which will redeem the situation."

"Then merely allow his lordship to do the talking. Answer only when it is required of you."

"He must think me a poor creature indeed."

"Recall that you are now Lady Astbury and through no wish of your own," the maid reminded her unnecessarily. "He cannot possibly lay the blame with you, ma'am."

"He will think no better of me for that. Not that he is the kind of man *I* would have chosen either. He is too much like Papa for my liking."

So saying she swept out of the room and down the stairs.

"The library, if you please," she demanded of the lackey in the hall. Gazing at her curiously he first knocked on the door and then thrust it open for her to enter.

Elyssa felt she was doing quite well but then the tension she was feeling made her cough, which spoiled it. The earl, who had been standing by the desk perusing some papers, looked up as she came slowly across the room.

"Good morning, Miss . . . er
. . . Elyssa."

"Being Countess of Astbury is exceeding odd to me, too," she answered, eyeing him warily.

"Well, there is nought to be done about it now."

"Surely there must be."

He frowned at her, surprised at this stance. "There is nothing I would wish to do." After a pause he asked, "Did you sleep well?"

She averted her eyes and seemed more retiring once again. "Yes, I thank you."

The lie did not fool him, for he had already noted her red-rimmed eyes. "Be pleased to sit down." She did so and he added, "I would also like you to accept my apology for my servants not knowing who you were last night . . . this morning."

"How could they? I expected no more. It was not my wish to come here."

The earl was beginning to feel

61

discomforted and he cleared his throat. "Well, it is done and I thought it might be prudent for you to leave London for a while. Accordingly I have made arrangements for you to go to my country house, which is in Bedfordshire, for a while. I am certain you will like it."

He thought about the desolate pile for a few moments and then put it from his mind quite determinedly. After all, the chit could not possibly stay in London, here in his house.

Smiling, he went on, "It really needs a good deal of renovation, but I don't believe you will find it uncomfortable."

She fixed him with an unexpectedly firm gaze. "When do I leave?"

"This morning, if it can be contrived. My man of business, Michael Bolton, will accompany you and attend to your comfort and safety on the journey. When your maid has packed . . . "

"It will not take long, I assure you. I have few vanities and fewer possessions, Lord Astbury."

He was even more discomforted. "Then I shall wish you a safe journey, Miss . . . er . . . Elyssa."

She got to her feet and turned to go. Suddenly he was moved to say, "I know this has all been as disappointing to you as it is to me. I hope you understand that a period of separation is necessary."

"And welcome," she added, smiling tightly. "What has happened is iniquitous to us both, Lord Astbury, but it will continue to happen whilst women are subject to a man's authority. A wife or a daughter is absolutely his own to do with as he pleases. Unless that changes, life will continue to be unbearable for many."

Astonished, he watched her sweep out of the room and when, at last, he returned his attention to the business in hand the footman came to announce the arrival of Charles Lamont.

The earl bit back a gasp of exasperation. "My trials are not yet over, it seems, but he will be a worried man this morning, I feel." He looked to the lackey. "Very well; you had better show him in."

Quickly, he pushed all his papers into a drawer before sitting down with his boots resting on the desk as if nothing had ever vexed him.

5

LORD ASTBURY perused a handful of bills before turning to his man of business. "A very satisfactory state of affairs, Bolton. Do you not think so, too?"

"Your financial situation, my lord, is vastly improved."

"It could scarce grow worse, despite unsecured loans to my father-in-law," the earl added grimly. "I fear I not only acquired an unwanted wife but a financial liability in her father."

The man looked discomforted. "Do you wish me to press for payment, my lord?"

"It would be a total waste of your time. Refuse him further loans, Bolton. I shall not be available if he approaches me, as I am certain he will. Is there any further business which needs my attention?"

"Just these, my lord."

He pushed a sheaf of vouchers in front of the earl. Frowning, he sifted through them.

"Masonry, timber, glass, carpet, furnishing fabrics? The tradesmen's bills were settled months ago for the work they did here so what the devil . . . ?"

"It's her ladyship, my lord. All these come from tradesmen in the area around Chipping Park."

The earl slammed them down on the desk. "What can she be about, I wonder?"

"Possibly her ladyship is having a few essential repairs carried out, my lord," Bolton suggested.

"A few! My dear fellow, from the amounts involved she must be renovating the entire house."

"The repairs are necessary, if I may venture to say so, my lord."

"That is certainly true, Bolton, but no one gave Lady Astbury leave to have them carried out."

"The house is in quite an appalling state, my lord, although it hardly mattered when only servants were in residence." The earl gave him a cold look which didn't daunt the fellow. "If you're concerned, perchance you would like me to ride out and inspect the place for you."

The earl gazed at him for a few moments before answering, "I think not. It would be inappropriate. I shall go myself. I fail to imagine Lady Astbury running up such expense. Such extravagance is totally out of character. Make the necessary arrangements and I shall leave within the sen'night."

"Do you wish me to accompany you, my lord?"

Glancing at him, the earl realized his man of business was a mite anxious to go to Chipping Park, and his eyes narrowed shrewdly.

"Tell me, Bolton, during your last journey to Chipping Park with Lady Astbury, what opinion did you form of her?" For once Bolton looked taken aback. "My lord . . . ?"

"You are capable of forming an opinion, are you not? 'Tis a simple enough question I put to you."

He averted his eyes from the earl's probing gaze. "She seemed exceeding unhappy, my lord, which in the circumstances was not undue, but that is all I was able to note during our journey."

"But surely you supped together?"

"I respected Lady Astbury's inclination not to talk."

"I had myself noted she had little to say for herself that was of any consequence."

"But, my lord, you must only allow for her circumstances at the time. A judgement in such circumstances could only have been misleading."

At such a hasty defence Lord Astbury sat back in his chair and eyed Michael Bolton wryly. "I believe you are smitten by her charms, Bolton, although I declare I never perceived any."

"No, my lord," was the noncommittal

reply, but a telling flush crept up in his cheek. With rather more haste than usual he gathered up some papers from the desk before bowing low in front of his master. "By your leave, my lord."

As he hurried out of the room, the earl watched him curiously, wondering how it was at all possible for any man to be enamoured of that poor creature.

* * *

From the comfort of her four poster bed and propped up by several lace-edged pillows, Sophia Fontwell gazed across the room.

"Really, Astbury, do you have to leave me so soon? Your haste is almost insulting."

Her lips curled petulantly. Her dark hair fanned out on the pillows, a perfect frame for her pale skin.

The earl, who had been gazing into a mirror whilst trying to tie his cravat, cast her a glance over his shoulder.

"I have urgent business at Chipping Park and plan to visit there at the earliest moment. In the meantime I have matters to attend to in Town."

"Oh, do you have to go just now?" she asked in a plaintive voice which rarely failed to move him.

"I am afraid I must."

"You'll be gone for weeks."

"I shall be gone no longer than absolutely necessary, but I do not have to ask your permission to do so."

"But you will miss me, won't you?"

He fastened a diamond pin to his cravat before turning to look at her properly. "You know I will, Sophia."

As if to illustrate the point he went to sit on the counterpane and gathered her into his arms, kissing her for a long time.

"I shall certainly miss you," she sighed when he released her at last.

"Your husband's attentions will have to suffice in my absence."

At this pronouncement Sophia laughed. "Even if he were here that couldn't possibly be so, but he's with his regiment somewhere in Norfolk at the moment. I only hope he will be obliged to stay there."

"Such wifely devotion," the earl mocked.

Sophia wound a dark curl around her finger. "I make no secret of my loathing of him. He's a beast. Our marriage was arranged by our parents and neither of us had a taste for it."

"A common lament, I fear."

"You, poor dear, fared as badly. It could hardly have been worse if you'd lost the wager."

"Not so, my dear; I might have lost the considerable amount of money I had won earlier in the evening."

"I am persuaded you would have preferred that to winning *Elyssa*. There could hardly be a misalliance greater than yours."

He took her hand and caressed it thoughtfully. "I believed *you* to be his daughter. If I had known . . ."

She gave him an encouraging smile.

71

"But now we are together far more than I am with Desmond and you enjoy my company more often than Elyssa's."

"I could scarce enjoy it less," he answered wryly.

"In any event you do have her two thousand a year. Many men have married for less."

"I required a great deal more and mayhap that is why I did not become legshackled earlier."

She chuckled. "Poor Papa. He was so chagrined because there was no way he could put his hands on the money. He never ceased to try."

"Does he still gamble?" the earl asked.

"Whenever he can raise a stake, which is not all that often of late."

"He approached me for a game of brag some weeks ago, but I told him I should only play if there was a chance he could win his daughter back."

Sophia threw back her head and laughed delightedly and then said, teasingly, "You really should make her your wife, Astbury."

Equally teasingly, he answered, "How do you know I did not?"

"You were together only one night."

"That was long enough."

She began to pout. "As if I care, but I shall loathe every moment you are with her at Chipping Park."

"You have no need to fear; my visit is a purely business affair."

She sank back into the pillows. "Is not Chipping Park close by Hartington Priory?"

He frowned. "A few miles away. Too close for my liking. Do you know of it, Sophia?"

"Only by repute. I was speaking with Sir Courteney Hartington only the other evening and he chanced to mention that my sister-in-law was in residence nearby his own country estate."

His eyes narrowed slightly and he looked far from pleased. "Did he indeed?"

She gave him another teasing look. "I've heard tell that he is a terribly wicked man. Is it true?"

"I am not well enough acquainted with the fellow to judge, but I dare say it is so. I cannot say I am much partial to his company."

"And is it also true that Hartington Priory is the home of the infamous Dalton Cloister which performs weird ceremonies by the light of the moon?"

"How should I know?" he asked, with mock outrage.

Her eyes sparkled with mischief. "As a close neighbour, I thought you might have been invited to partake of the ceremonies."

The earl continued to look outraged. "What kind of a man do you think I am, Sophia?"

"One who might well enjoy midnight revels in the ruined priory," she ventured. "After all, it could be quite diverting, I dare say."

"I do not need to dress up in a monk's habit, nor have a female wear a nun's robe to enjoy her company."

She looked at him from beneath her long, dark lashes. "So you do know about it after all."

He was beginning to display signs of irritation. "I hear the tattle in the coffee houses."

"There is a good deal of talk about him. I have even heard that a servant girl actually died during one evening's revels and that her family were paid handsomely by Sir Courteney to pretend it had occurred elsewhere."

The earl got to his feet, saying, "I know nothing about it, nor do I wish to, and my advice to you is not to become involved with Sir Courteney Hartington."

"You need not say so, my love; one rake at a time is quite enough for this poor creature."

She gave him a coy look and he replied, as he carefully put on his coat, "You're remarkably modest today, my dear."

She gave a sudden gasp of exasperation

as he prepared to take his leave of her. "Are you truly going only on business?"

"Truly," he assured her. "The estate is in a shocking condition and it is time I turned my attention to putting it to rights."

"With your wife's money."

He cast her a warning look. "Sophia, my wife has no money; it is all mine."

"You men are so arrogant."

He reached out and fingered the matched pearls which encircled her throat. "I think you do well out of men, arrogant or not, my dear."

"You'll be horrendously bored," she accused.

"Yes, I dare say I shall, but," he added, casting her a smile, "thoughts of you will sustain me until we meet again."

He came back to the bed to place a light kiss on her forehead and she clung to him for a few moments before he pulled away determinedly.

"Life will be devilishly dull without you, Astbury."

"At least you shall have the diversions of London to enjoy whilst I'm gone."

She chuckled and added for him. "Whereas you shall have only Elyssa."

He looked at her with sudden interest then. "Are you not fond of your sister-in-law?"

"Exceeding, but I am the first to admit she is not the most diverting company."

"That was my own impression and I wonder if it was erroneous."

"It certainly is not, although I found her an odd creature to understand. Lady Fontwell was always used to treating her as a servant. Fetch my sewing, Elyssa, bring me that shawl," she mimicked. "I declare Lady Fontwell is quite lost without her."

The earl stood at the end of the bed. "At the time of our marriage I gained the distinct impression that she was exceeding sickly."

"She has a lung complaint but I always had a suspicion that she was stronger than she appeared."

"That does support my own feeling now," he answered thoughtfully. "When Elyssa went down to Chipping Park I did send a note to the local physician to be ready at any time for a summons, but so far I have received no bills from him and must assume he has not called upon her."

"To give her due credit, Astbury, she was never one to complain. She abhorred fuss and I believe she would have to be dying before she would allow a physician to be called. I am only surprised she has lived so long. Several eminent physicians, including a Jew from Leyden, declared her a hopeless case. Of course they bleed her from time to time, but all their ministrations, blisters, poultices and so on have not helped. This has been going on as long as I recall. She must be all of three and twenty now, you know."

"I didn't," he answered, still thoughtful.

He knew almost nothing about her,

save that she was an unwanted burden even with her two thousand pounds a year, but Sophia's remarks did cause him to reflect about Elyssa's state of health. He wondered what condition he would discover her in after six months in the country, and experienced a small stab of guilt for not thinking of it earlier. Over the previous months he had been so besotted with Sophia he had scarce had a chance to think of anything or anyone else, nor had he wanted to, certainly not the cards which had brought him so much affluence.

He picked up his stick, hat and gloves before blowing her a kiss.

"Shall I see you before you leave for Chipping Park?" she asked. "Oh, surely you can spare an hour for me?"

"If it is at all possible, but I know I shall be busy. However, we shall certainly see each other as soon as it is possible. You may rely upon that, my dear."

"Perchance sooner than you think," she murmured as she watched the door close behind him.

The moment he had gone she flung back the bedclothes and wrapped a silk peignoir around her ample curves. She sat down at an escritoire at the far side of the room, deep in thought for several minutes before a smile touched her lips again. Drawing a sheet of parchment towards her, she picked up a quill and after only a moment's hesitation she dipped it into the ink and began to write.

6

THE carriage, emblazoned with the coat of arms of the Earl of Astbury, bowled up the beech avenue leading to Chipping Park at a spanking pace.

The house had been built in the time of Henry Tudor, but it had undergone several changes since then under successive occupiers. However, the last one had visited his country estate but once in his lifetime, allowing it to fall victim to neglect thereafter.

On acceding to the title the present earl had, of course, visited the house with very great expectations, but, after seeing the scale of renovation which would be necessary to put it to rights, he had departed again, feeling he would never be in funds sufficiently nor of the right heart to do all that was necessary to give the house the correct degree of comfort to make it habitable again.

With growing dismay he had seen room after room where damp had penetrated the plasterwork, ruining the decoration. Much of the furniture had fallen foul of the worm, carpets were threadbare, inviting disaster to all who stepped unwarily. At every window the curtains hung filthy and half off the rails, and the odour of must and decay had lingered in his nostrils long after he had departed. The new Lord Astbury had remained but one night and much like his predecessor he had not thought to come again.

Despite the degree of dilapidation he had encountered, sending Elyssa to Chipping Park had not caused his conscience to prick as he considered there were rooms enough for the comfort of one person and staff sufficient to care for her needs. The earl had been quite convinced that an establishment of her own, however decrepit, must be preferable to the life she had led in the heart of her rather dreadful family.

The sun was shining on the window panes in the numerous mullions as he approached, and for the first time, when he peered out of the carriage windows, Lord Astbury thought it was quite an attractive place. It was certainly better than his neighbour's house, which boasted a ruined priory in the gardens and yet the house itself, unlike Chipping Park, was of no architectural merit.

The carriage drew to a halt in front of the shallow flight of steps which led to the portico and main entrance. The moment the footman let down the steps the earl climbed down, immediately turning to take in the view of the formal gardens, unchanged for two centuries and which sloped down to an ornamental lake.

As he gazed at the pleasing vista the earl suddenly realized that somehow it was not quite the same as when he had last visited. It was immediately apparent that the gardens were far more orderly than they previously were. No longer were they choked with weeds, no more overgrown borders blighted the view. On his last visit the lake had been choked with weeds, too, but this appeared to have been rectified also. Broken and fallen statues had been replaced or righted, and even the trees seemed to have taken on an altogether neater silhouette. All was neat and orderly, and there was a pleasing display of early summer flowers in all the beds and borders.

At the same time as he admired the view, the earl also became aware of some distant sounds disturbing what would otherwise have been a peaceful idyll. From somewhere not too far away came the chink of a mallet on stone, the sound of sawing wood. He turned and saw that a man dressed in Astbury livery, scarlet with silver frogging, was hurrying towards him from the direction of the house.

On reaching the earl, the servant

bowed low, "Allardice, my lord. Your house-steward."

"What has happened to Fenton?" came the sharp question.

"Lady Astbury considered he should be retired, my lord, and engaged me in his stead. May I escort you inside? I most heartily beg your pardon, my lord, for the disarray, only your note arrived only an hour ago."

The earl felt a stirring of irritation. "It was dispatched in good time, I assure you. Now, where is her ladyship?" he asked abruptly, making no move to go inside as more servants than he recalled removed his trunks from the second carriage which had arrived in the wake of the first.

"As I said, my lord, your note arrived only an hour ago. Lady Astbury was out at the time and has not yet returned."

"Out! Where on earth has she gone?"

"Riding, my lord, as is her custom at this time of the day."

The earl cast him a ferocious look.

"When is she expected to return?"

"At any time now, my lord."

No sooner had he spoken than a gig could be seen moving between the beeches and along the drive. The earl cast the servant a cool look. "That will be all for now, Allardice. You may go and I shall await Lady Astbury's arrival myself."

The man bowed low and hurried back inside, no doubt to supervise the delivering of the trunks.

The earl stood on the top step, his hands clasped behind his back as the gig came nearer to the house. He followed its progress with keen interest.

The countess was driving it herself, but there was a thin, disreputable-looking mongrel dog at her side. As the gig drew up abreast of the earl's two carriages he noted the look of amazement and alarm which came upon her face. She handed the reins to a waiting footman and climbed down quickly. She was wearing a simple gown of green tabby, a chipstraw hat hiding most of her reddish hair, the earl noted and although her simplicity of style had changed little since his last sight of her she seemed to possess more substance than he recalled. She paused in front of the gig, casting him a look which was both fearful and questioning and when he made no move to greet her she came slowly towards him as if every step was an effort to her. He stared down at her forbiddingly, but she had only just started forward when the mongrel sprang towards him, barking and snarling in a most alarming way.

The countess looked even more flustered as she called, "Tinker! Oh, Tinker, do come back."

The dog ignored her pleading completely and in the wake of the attack the earl drew back, saying, "Call off the brute!"

"I am trying to do so. Tinker! Oh, Tinker, you are a very bad boy!"

The mongrel pawed at the earl's breeches as he cried, "Down, down

I say! Have you no control over this animal?"

Distressed, she called to one of the footmen who grabbed at the dog's leather leash and managed to drag him away at last.

The earl watched him go with distaste as his wife said breathlessly, "Oh, Astbury, I am so sorry."

"And so you should be. What is that creature?"

"I am not quite certain, but he is normally quite harmless. I cannot think what has caused him to behave so badly."

"Forgive me if I find that hard to believe," he replied, brushing at the muddy pawmarks the dog had deposited on his breeches. "I don't recall seeing him here before and I am persuaded I should."

"He has been here only a short while," she explained, evidently embarrassed.

He looked up slowly and met her eyes which she immediately averted. "He was ill-treated by his former master, an itinerant tinker who called here one day. I took pity on the poor creature and persuaded the vile owner to part with him, and he has been devoted to me ever since. Perchance you remind him of his former master and that is why he is so perturbed."

The earl shot her a cold look. "I am the one who is perturbed, madam. By what means did you persuade this fellow to part with his dog?"

"I gave him half a guinea."

"Half a guinea! The wretch will be back on the doorstep within a sen'night with another wild creature."

"Which I shall have to buy from him, I fear."

"On the contrary, madam, this one will have to go if his fancy is to attack me."

"I am certain he will not do so again," she answered hastily. "At least . . . I shall make certain he is kept out of your way."

"Be sure that you do, for I mean

what I say. I have not come all the way from London with no mishap to be attacked by a mad dog on my own doorstep."

"You need have no fear. Now," she sighed, "this is quite a shock to me, Astbury. I did not look to see you here."

He looked grim. So far his arrival had been far from how he'd imagined it to be. He'd expected to discover his wife a considerable invalid by now and finding her in no such state served to discompose him greatly.

"Evidently," he snapped. "However, my note did arrive an hour ago when you were out."

"Oh, indeed, that is most unfortunate, I own, but I always ride on all but the most atrocious days."

His eyes narrowed. "Where in heavens' name do you ride?"

Breathlessly she answered, "Everywhere. Sometimes I go on horseback and occasionally in the gig."

"Have you always done so?"

"No. I have rarely resided in the country before."

She averted her eyes as he went on, "Then this is a sudden whim which has afflicted you?"

Keeping her eyes averted she explained, "I have what I deem to be a good reason."

"Which is?" he asked, his manner still cold and forbidding. She made no answer to that and he insisted, "Your reason, madam?"

In a quiet voice which he could scarcely hear she replied, "My retirement immediately after our wedding could I believe give rise to odd rumours." When she stole a glance at him he was still looking at her interrogatively. "I had no wish for the county to believe you had an insane wife hidden here at Chipping Park. *On dits* start so easily."

Her explanation seemed so absurd to him that he was obliged to fight his laughter. Instead he took a deep breath and answered, "I see. I do hope the county is relieved to find you quite sane."

"Shall we go inside?" she asked quickly.

Before he could answer she gathered up her skirts and preceded him into the house. As he followed he noted that her figure had become more rounded since he had last seen her and far from the damp country air making a speedy end to her, she seemed to be thriving on it.

He stepped into the hall and gazed around him in amazement for the panelling had been restored to its former beauty and the glass chandelier gleamed where it was once grimy and lifeless.

"Well, there is quite a difference," he declared, not entirely with approval.

"You will find many such improvements throughout the house," she ventured, eyeing him warily again.

"You seem set upon surprising me, Elyssa."

She gave him a resentful look as he

stripped off his gloves. "I think none of it will be a surprise to you, my lord."

The sounds of sawing and banging were louder now they had entered the house, and the countess moved quickly away from him.

"You must excuse me if everything is not to your liking as yet. The house is not as it should be and still full of workmen. They will not be hurried even if I had been given prior warning of your arrival."

"We shall discuss the matter at length later," he told her, his tone ominous. "In the meantime I would like to go up to my room and wash away a little of the grime of an uncomfortable journey."

Her hand flapped in the air. "Of course. Only . . . " He raised one eyebrow questioningly and she went on in a breathless voice again, "The bedchambers are the last rooms to be renovated. I never expected visitors, you see . . . "

"I am not a visitor. I own this

house. You do have a bedchamber fit for habitation, do you not?"

"Oh, yes, only we do have another guest . . . "

His eyes narrowed. "I am not a guest, Elyssa, but pray do tell me whom you are entertaining."

"She only arrived yesterday. I could not refuse. The poor dear was so miserable whilst Desmond is away with his regiment . . . "

The earl stared at her in dawning disbelief but before he could speak a voice from the stairs cried, "Lord Astbury! *Quelle surprise!* My sister-in-law didn't tell me you were expected."

The earl swung round on his heel to see none other than Sophia Fontwell standing halfway down the stairs, looking exquisite in a gown of burgundy velvet. She had paused on many a staircase, aware of the effect the sight of her usually had on gentlemen present, not to mention the envy she inspired in their ladies.

However, on this occasion the sight

of her filled the earl with a passion of a different kind to the one to which he was accustomed. He was quite simply furious, firstly with his wife for the changes she had made to the house without prior permission, and with Sophia for arriving with no warning to him.

Elyssa said in a muted tone, "I believe, my lord, you have already met my brother's wife, Mrs Fontwell."

"Indeed I have," he replied and his voice betrayed nothing of the ire he was feeling. Only his eyes betrayed his chagrin.

He went forward as Sophia came slowly down the stairs. "Welcome to Chipping Park, Mrs Fontwell. I trust my wife has made you comfortable."

"Very much so, Lord Astbury."

As he took her hand and raised it to his lips she bobbed a curtsey. When he raised his eyes to hers he saw there was a look of triumph in them. However, her voice was filled with a convincing innocence.

"Had I known you were to come, my lord, I would not have imposed upon your wife's hospitality at this time."

"Oh, nonsense, Sophia!" Elyssa chided. "His lordship doesn't mind in the least."

He did not gainsay her. He simply bowed to them both and went slowly up the stairs, his heart filled with fury at Sophia's underhand behaviour. It was the first time he had felt anything but infatuation for her since they first met.

7

FACED with the prospect of dining with his wife and his mistress at one and the same time, the earl looked forward to the meal with no gusto. However, no sooner had he joined the two ladies in the small salon, repaired and redecorated with surprisingly excellent taste — he could quarrel with no part of it — then the footman came to announce the arrival of Sir Courteney Hartington, Mrs Kitty Lamont and Mr Charles Lamont.

"What the . . . ?"

Elyssa put one hand to her head. "Oh dear! The excitement of your arrival put it quite out of my head."

He cast her a scathing look. "Then pray acquaint me with the facts with no further delay."

Sophia reclined on a sofa, a smile

playing about her lips, and she seemed not at all daunted by her lover's cool reception of her.

Elyssa twisted her hands together. "I do beg your pardon, my lord, only I had no notion you would be coming."

"So you keep saying," he answered irritably.

"Sir Courteney is our nearest neighbour and has called on several occasions since I arrived. He has been most charming, I own, and when Sophia intimated a desire to meet him, I thought to invite him to dinner. And then a Mrs Lamont called in — a guest at the Priory, it seems. She told me she was your closest relative, so I needs must include her."

"Closest, but not close," the earl amended.

Elyssa was wide-eyed. "She has acquainted me with the fact that her son is your heir."

He took a pinch of snuff and replied as he snapped the box lid shut, "Now perhaps, but that is not to say for ever."

Elyssa's cheeks grew pink and she went on, "I deemed it only correct to invite him, too. I hope I have not displeased you, at least no more than is usual," she added lamely.

That last statement startled him and after a moment he said grudgingly, "They are a trio of prosy bores." He nodded to the footman. "Show them in."

"I suspect Lord Astbury wished to have your company to himself on his first evening at Chipping Park," Sophia teased, giving him a knowing glance.

Her reward was a cold look from the earl as the guests were ushered into the salon.

Sir Courteney Hartington, tall and thin and dressed exquisitely in a coat of gold damask, his face heavily powdered and patched, immediately made a sweeping bow which encompassed them all.

"My dear Lady Astbury," he

immediately went to kiss her hand, "how delightful you look this evening, but 'tis no more than I have come to expect of one who possesses such incredibly exquisite taste." With rather less enthusiasm he bowed to the earl. "Your servant, Astbury."

He was rewarded by a cool nod from his unwilling host.

"La! What a surprise to find you in residence," declared Kitty Lamont as she swept into the room.

The earl dutifully raised her hand to his lips. "Am I not wont to spring surprises?"

She gave him a playful tap with her fan. "And almost always they are delightful ones, I own."

"Sir Courteney, Mrs Lamont, Mr Lamont," said Elyssa in a quiet voice, "allow me to present my brother's wife, Mrs Fontwell."

"I am enchanted," Sir Courteney immediately declared. "Rusticating has always been such a trial, but now, I declare, all is changed!"

"I am delighted to make the acquaintance of the infamous Sir Courteney Hartington," she replied coquettishly, giving him a speculative look from beneath her lashes. "I have heard so many stories about you."

"Undoubtedly false ones, dear lady, but do tell me all about them. I am always agog to hear what is being said of me in the salons of the *ton*."

He seated himself next to Sophia and immediately engaged her in an animated conversation. Mrs Lamont lowered herself into an armless chair which accommodated her huge skirts whilst her son retreated sulkily to a corner to glare at them all.

"A glass of ratafia?" the earl asked before giving the footman the signal to hand around the tray.

"When we spoke yesterday," Mrs Lamont ventured, eyeing him curiously, "dear Lady Astbury made no mention of your imminent arrival."

"She did not know of it, Cousin Kitty. There have been surprises all round and, I trust," he glanced at his wife whose eyes were downcast, "this is the last of them."

Mrs Lamont took her glass of ratafia and after having a sizeable sip went on, "How odd it is to see you of all people well settled into matrimony, Astbury."

"Matrimony is something all of us indulge in at some time or other. It is usually to be recommended highly."

"Indeed and I do declare it becomes you."

The earl bestowed a charming smile upon her. "I am so glad you think so, Kitty."

"It becomes Lady Astbury even more. I declare she looks quite a different person to the one I recall in London."

The earl transferred his attention to his wife, for Kitty Lamont had echoed exactly his own thoughts. Not only had Elyssa become more rounded, her complexion had an altogether more healthy hue to it and he had yet to hear one of those debilitating bouts of coughing which had so often afflicted her in London.

"I have noted that myself," he replied.

Elyssa looked pleased. When she smiled her cheeks dimpled and her eyes seemed to be a curious shade of green in the candlelight. Her red-hued hair took on a burnished look, enhanced by the green velvet gown she wore. It was of an unfashionable cut and yet it became her more than the modish gowns worn by the two other ladies present.

"'Tis true, I own," she replied, happily clutching at her glass of ratafia. "I feel quite a different person since coming to Chipping Park."

"Do allow us the secret of your recovery," Mrs Lamont begged with some asperity evident in her tone.

"I am not at all certain that I can," the countess replied, casting her husband an occasional uncertain glance as he gazed at her expressionlessly. "I am persuaded the good country air

103

has been beneficial to me whereas the smoky atmosphere in Town did not agree with me at all. Mrs Carmichael, the housekeeper I appointed when I arrived, is a true countrywoman and she has made many a tisane for me since I took up residence here."

Mrs Lamont transferred her attention to the earl. "Astbury, you are indebted to this woman."

"Indeed," he answered quietly, finishing his drink.

Glancing around, Mrs Lamont murmured, "How congenial this gathering is, I declare, and how fortunate Charles and I intend to stay at Hartington Priory a little while longer which will enable us to meet often."

She cast the earl a contented look but he only appeared to be chagrined, something noted by his wife whose spirits sank to an even greater depth.

Sir Courteney left Sophia's side at last and went to join Elyssa where he could immediately be seen flattering her unceasingly. Although Mrs Lamont endeavoured to interrupt frequently her attempts met with little success. The earl put down his half-filled glass and took the opportunity of joining Sophia who was now sitting alone on the sofa.

"I was persuaded you were going to ignore me throughout my stay," she told him as he sat down.

"How else should I behave towards a woman I claim only to know very slightly?"

"With a little more cordiality, at least."

"Mayhap you think I should make love to you in full view of everyone present."

She gazed into his eyes. "If you did, I assure you I should not be aware of anyone but you."

He bit back a gasp of annoyance. "Sophia, you seem not to have realized I am really very angry with you for coming here."

Not put out, she answered, "I know, but your anger towards me cannot

105

possibly last and you will soon grow glad that I am here."

"Unfortunately I shall not have the opportunity. You have conveniently forgotten that I am here on business."

"Not every moment. Not now, for instance," she crooned, smiling across at Elyssa who cast them anxious looks from time to time.

When she returned her attention to the earl, he said, "Tomorrow you will make some excuse to my wife and leave."

At this the woman looked astounded. Her confident smile faded abruptly and she recoiled from him as if he had struck her.

"I do not believe you mean that."

He fixed her with a stare which brooked no argument. "I always mean what I say, Sophia."

With an angry frown she looked away. "You are very ungallant."

"And you must be as mad as May butter to come here so brazenly," he whispered angrily. "I will not have my

106

mistress and my wife beneath the same roof."

Her eyes flashed with considerable anger. "How dare you class me as one of your common doxies!"

Unmoved by her anger and able to control his own much better he took a pinch of snuff and as he returned the box to his pocket replied, "What else would you term yourself, my dear?"

Her hand jerked and he realized she was longing to slap him. He caught Charles Lamont's eye and smiled at the fellow before returning his attention to Sophia whose breast was heaving beneath the silk bodice of her gown.

She looked away, evidently attempting to control her anger and frustration. "Even though you insult me I do not wish to quarrel with you."

"Nor I with you, be assured, so please be an obedient wench and do as I ask."

"I thought you would be pleased to see me. I am sorely disappointed, Astbury."

"For that I am truly sorry, my dear, but you must see your presence here can only cause unlooked for complications."

"I cannot in all conscience conceive why. If it is Elyssa who concerns you, she must know you do not live the life of a saint in London."

"In London," he echoed. "What I do and whom I see in London is a different matter."

"I cannot see why."

"I am not asking that you should, my dear."

"Oh, I could not bear the thought of being without you, even be it for a sen'night. I was so miserable at the thought of being alone."

"Nevertheless I did not give you leave to come here. You should have asked."

"To what purpose, I wonder? You would have merely refused me permission."

"Precisely."

"I cannot go so soon," she said in

desperation. "In my letter I specified a stay of at least a sen'night, and if I go now she will blame your presence which I am sure you do not want." She laughed and for the first time the sound irritated him. "Elyssa is quite persuaded we dislike each other heartily. My departure will only cause her untold anguish."

He drew in a sharp breath through his teeth, struggling to keep his anger from spilling over. "Very well; you may stay, but I shall not forgive you so soon."

She gave him a coquettish look. "Tush. Come to my room later and we shall see how soon you forget my little transgression."

"If you really wish to be of service to me, contrive to monopolize Sir Courteney's attention. He is being far too familiar with my wife."

She cast him a curious look. "You are surely not jealous, Astbury?"

For once he was startled and then he retorted, "Certainly not, but you are more equipped to deal with a rake such as he. Elyssa can have no notion."

She chuckled then, her anger forgotten. "From the look of her I would say she has learned a great deal of late."

To his further annoyance that appeared to be so. Elyssa was laughing at some remark Sir Courteney had made, and she had his total attention. Her face was quite animated and her eyes bright. The repulsive paleness was gone from her cheeks which now bloomed with health. Sitting there responding to Courteney Hartington's flirting, the earl considered her almost fetching.

Charles Lamont had noted it, too. He seated himself at his mother's side saying, "Lady Astbury seems not at all the person you led me to believe, Mamma. What was that Banbury Tale you told me about her being sickly and not like to live for long?"

" 'Twas true, I vow. She hides it well,

110

that is all. Paint hides a great deal for all of us."

"I don't believe she wears any, Mamma, and only look how men fawn upon her."

"Oh, tush. What does it matter? For a six month, since the night of their marriage, they have lived apart. Since then, Sir Courteney tells me, he has flirted with her unceasingly at every turn. Her youth and innocence is a magnet to him."

"That is hardly a comfort to me, Mamma."

"Your whining bores me, Charles. You must sit back and enjoy yourself for this situation is charged with amusement."

"You must forgive me, but I cannot see that."

"Sophia Fontwell is at present Astbury's favourite *chère amie*. Now do you see? La! What a splendid diversion this is!"

She was still laughing merrily when the earl came to take her into dinner.

As she got to her feet she told him, "I was just remarking to Charles what a perfect party this is, Astbury."

He smiled faintly. "My dear Cousin Kitty, I am persuaded that is only because you are here."

She laughed again and glanced over her shoulder to see Elyssa being escorted by Sir Courteney, causing her to cast a knowing look at her son who managed to smile with satisfaction at last.

8

ELYSSA sat at the dressing table, gazing into the mirror, the reflection of her own face flickering in the candlelight and fireglow. Her maid pulled the last pin out of her hair and her curls fell past her shoulders and framed her face which had taken on a now unaccustomed pallor.

"Your hair is so pretty now, ma'am," her maid commented.

"That concoction of eggs which Mrs Carmichael prepared for me certainly has improved its texture," Elyssa mused as she fingered a curl pensively.

"And the strawberry water has done wonders for your complexion, too, ma'am."

The countess sighed. "I am so glad tonight is over, Dora. It was an ordeal. I have never played hostess before. I would not mind only Lord Astbury always looks so angry and I know he was displeased with my guests although 'twas not my fault he arrived today. He does not like Sir Courteney who is charm itself to me."

"All the more reason for you to like him, ma'am," the maid replied, brushing her mistress's hair with long sweeping strokes.

"I own I do like being made to feel pretty, Dora, but perchance that is only because it has never happened to me before."

"You are pretty, ma'am, really you are. Now your health's improved you look quite handsome."

"Is it wrong of me to want to be admired?"

"No, ma'am. What else is there for a fine lady except to be admired? All married ladies of quality have their gallants."

"Yes, I know, but I am not yet a wife, Dora. If only Lord Astbury would look upon me more favourably!

The situation as it is at present is most frustrating. Oh, I know he could never love me so that fact does not plague me at all. So few men do love their wives, I know, although it is a woman's place to love her husband, come what may, and I would wish to be a good spouse if he would only let me."

"You're too good for the likes of him, that's what you are, ma'am."

Elyssa gave the girl a sharp look. "You mustn't say such a wicked thing, Dora. I will not countenance such talk."

The girl bit her lip. "Beg pardon, ma'am, but you don't deserve being pushed out here in the country and ignored."

"It's an arrangement which suits us both. Lord Astbury does not want me in London and I am quite content to remain here. It has been the best time of my life, Dora, truly it has."

The maidservant smiled. "Yes, I know, ma'am."

"The problems only arise when he comes here."

"Happen it won't be too often and mayhap he'll be gone again soon," the maid suggested cheerfully.

Elyssa sighed deeply. "Oh, yes, Dora, let us hope that is so."

There came a knock on the door which caused Elyssa's contented smile to fade. Dora put down the brush and went to open the door. It was Sophia who stood there, carrying a candle and she was wrapped in a silk peignoir which did nothing to hide her ample curves.

"Sophia," Elyssa gasped in astonishment, "is there anything amiss?"

Her sister-in-law smiled faintly. "No, no, 'tis only that I didn't expect to find you here."

"Pray who did you expect to find here?"

Sophia became suddenly flustered. "I didn't mean that. What I meant was I didn't expect to find you in dishabille."

"*You* are."

The woman flushed faintly in the candlelight. "Why, yes . . . I was undressing when I realized I felt not the least sleepy and wondered if you would like a coze."

"Of course, Sophia. Do come in and sit by the fire."

A look of relief crossed her face as she came into the room. Elyssa gave her a curious look before turning to her maid and saying quickly, "You may retire now, Dora."

"Shall I take out the warming pan, my lady?"

"Yes, please do."

The maid removed the warming pan from the bed and left it by the fire. She cast Mrs Fontwell one last disapproving look before leaving the two women together, seated by the fire.

"Now, what is it you wish us to talk about?" asked Elyssa who likewise felt not the least like sleeping.

After a moment's hesitation Sophia ventured. "It was a congenial evening, was it not?"

"I am glad you enjoyed it," Elyssa replied noncommittally.

"Who could fail to be amused by Sir Courteney? He is reputed to be such a rake. A dangerous man, I should say." She eyed her sister-in-law speculatively before asking, "Are you well-acquainted with him?"

Elyssa shrugged. "We have ridden on occasions and he calls at the house now and again."

"I wonder why Astbury has chosen to visit just now." Again she gave Elyssa a speculative look.

"He does not confide in me, Sophia. However, there is no secret in the fact that the estate has been neglected for years and no doubt he is come to mend matters in that direction. You mustn't think he will interfere with any of our activities; your visit will not make any difference to what he has to do."

"I did feel that Lord Astbury would rather I wasn't here. My presence seemed to come as a severe shock to him. Do you think I should make arrangements to leave?"

"Of course I don't," Elyssa assured her, albeit uneasily. "I cannot conceive what has put such a thing into your head."

Sophia looked a picture of desolation. "Perchance I am too sensitive. It has often been said of me in the past."

"I am persuaded that you are in this instance. You mustn't mind him. Astbury can exert a deal of charm when he so chooses, but today, recall, he had endured an uncomfortable journey over terrible roads."

"How well I know that." Sophia smiled hesitantly. "Did I not travel the very same road not four and twenty hours earlier? You have relieved my mind considerably, for in truth I had no wish to return to Town so soon. It is devilishly dull with Desmond in Norfolk and I have so enjoyed your company which I miss sorely now you seem set to rusticate permanently."

"I am so glad," Elyssa told her happily. "Astbury has come on business so we shall neither of us see him much whilst he is here."

"It is such a dull task 'tis no wonder he is in such a disagreeable mood. Perchance Sir Courteney and Mr Lamont will ride over now and again and relieve our own boredom. They are such diverting company."

"I am certain that they will."

"In any event Sir Courteney would not wish to stay away from you so long," Sophia said coyly and Elyssa blushed.

She was glad of an end to that particular topic of conversation when the door opened again. However, she was not much pleased to see the earl, slightly the worse for drink and swaying in the doorway.

Immediately both women were on their feet as he looked at them both in disbelief.

"I shall bid you a goodnight," Sophia murmured, bobbing a curtsey and hurrying from the room. As she passed the earl she gave him a flirtatious look which he returned with an expressionless stare.

The door closed behind her and he peered at his wife across the room. Aware that she wore only a shift Elyssa drew a shawl about her.

"What are you doing here?" he demanded.

"I am about to retire," she answered softly, lowering her eyes modestly.

"Not here surely."

She raised her eyes again. "Yes."

"This is my room."

"Surely it is ours."

"Yours is through there," he said with an angry wave of his hand towards the communicating door, "if you feel it necessary to keep up the pretence of our felicity. For myself I really couldn't care."

Slowly and not taking her eyes from him, she picked up a candlestick and went towards the door. When she opened it he could see quite plainly the planks of wood and scaffolding which took up the entire room.

"Hell and damnation! You cannot mean to tell me there is no other room available in a house this size. There must be another."

"None of them were fit for use. I gave orders for them all to be renovated, not knowing that anyone else would require one. All the bedchambers are in a like condition, save for the one my sister-in-law occupies. It was mine before she arrived. This one had just been completed. Do you wish me to join her?"

The earl looked furious. He snatched up the candle from her hand, making her start. "You're a scheming woman, Elyssa, but it won't do."

"Scheming?" she asked in bewilderment, clutching the shawl about her. "I cannot conceive what you may mean by that."

He cast her a mocking look. "I wonder what truly lurks beneath that facade of innocence?"

He snatched at the shawl she had clutched about her something which caused her to jump back in alarm. He laughed, tossing the shawl back at her. "Nothing. Nothing at all. I cannot say that I'm surprised," he sneered.

She backed away further, hurriedly wrapping the shawl about her again. "I shall leave immediately. You may have the room to yourself."

"Don't trouble. This is a minor inconvenience as opposed to gaining an unwanted wife which is a monumental one. I shall have my valet bring in a truckle bed."

Tears welled up in her eyes as he opened the adjoining door again. "It is hard to be hated through no fault of one's own," she told him in a soft voice.

He paused to glance at her again. "'Tis late, Elyssa. Join me in the library at noon. Then you and I shall have that talk at last."

"I cannot — not at noon," she answered after hesitating fearfully.

He paused in the doorway, turning

slowly to look at her. She waited fearfully for the expected explosion of anger.

"Do tell me what pressing social event prevents you."

She swallowed nervously. "Every week I give lessons in reading and writing to some of the estate children."

His face suffused with colour. "What! Am I hearing you right?"

She looked away. "Yes."

"Why? Tell me why you have embarked upon this madcap scheme, Elyssa, before I decide you are a mad-woman."

"Oh, for heaven's sake! There is nothing mad about it."

He was suddenly sober, menacingly so. "I beg to differ," he said coldly and it was Elyssa's anger which was stimulated now.

"Pray tell me why should they not learn to read and write as we do?"

"Because they are not as we are," he answered, speaking each word slowly never taking his eyes from her face.

"Then tell me why we have the right and not they."

"They do not need to read and write to pull a plough or milk a cow."

Indignant now and oblivious to all else she retorted, "Perchance they will wish to do something other than that. I am sorry if you are displeased but some of the children come for miles across the fields and I cannot disappoint them."

"So I must be made to wait instead. Do you not consider my anger justified? Where are these lessons held?"

"Here in the house."

"Here! You must truly be a madwoman."

Her eyes flashed with anger. "If that is so it can hardly affect you. We live entirely separate lives and you are disassociated with everything I do."

"Not everything," he answered in a quiet but resolute voice. "I insist upon your maintaining the dignity of your position."

"I am sorry if you believe teaching

125

a few children to read and to write lowers the dignity of my position."

"Dammit, I do, madam."

She stood up straight. "Am I to take it you forbid me to continue?"

He drew in a sigh. "Would you obey me if I did?"

After hesitating a moment she replied, "I should be obliged to, but I take leave to warn you I would take it ill."

"When those children begin to question their place in Society it will be meddling females like you who'll be held responsible."

Frostily she asked, "Do I take it I may continue?"

"Until I see an adverse affect in any way, you may."

"I should be finished by two o'clock," she ventured and she was answered by the slamming of the door.

After staring at the closed door for several seconds Elyssa turned away. Feeling suddenly cold, she rubbed her arms and then, sinking on to the bed, she drew a deep sigh, wondering how, in the face of such mutual dislike and unresolved differences, it was all likely to end.

★ ★ ★

The sun was quite warm, trapped in the walled garden behind the house. Elyssa sat on one of the garden seats, an unopened book on her lap. Her mind was too full of uncomfortable thoughts to concentrate on the written word which she normally enjoyed so much.

Over the past six months she had not been obliged to give much thought to her marriage, nor had she wished to. Her most earnest desire was to forget the humiliating circumstances which led to her becoming the Countess of Astbury.

It had seemed clear at the time that the earl wished only to be rid of her and she was resigned to spending the rest of her life at Chipping Park. That was something which only pleased her, but now he had arrived and it seemed matters were not so simple. If only, she thought, I could be certain he will leave soon and not return.

Suddenly a footstep on the path caused her to start out of the maelstrom of the thoughts which were afflicting her at that moment. Tinker, who had been dozing at her feet sat up and began to bark. However, when she looked up she began to smile, for it was not, after all, her husband who intruded.

"Sir Courteney, you startled me, but what a pleasant surprise! I did not look to see you here today."

He looked askance at the dog and Elyssa said, "Do be silent, Tinker." The dog obeyed but continued to eye the newcomer suspiciously. "You mustn't mind Tinker," she begged, "even if he is overzealous."

Sir Courteney smiled hesitantly. "On the contrary, Lady Astbury, I envy him his role as your loyal servant." He looked at her then. "I hesitate to disturb you, my lady."

"I only wonder you found me."

"In the normal way I would not, but you have obliging servants."

She laughed. "They are well aware that this is my own little sanctuary."

"I am surprised you feel you need one, my lady."

"We all do; somewhere to retreat from the world and be alone with one's thoughts."

"I am, therefore, more than ever hesitant to spoil the idyll."

"Be assured that you are always welcome, even here. Won't you sit down?"

"Delighted."

He drew out a perfumed handkerchief and held it up to his face. "Mrs Fontwell has gone riding with Mr Lamont," Elyssa informed him.

"It was I, Lady Astbury, who entreated him to do so in the hope that I might solicit a few moments alone with you."

"How flattering, Sir Courteney! What do you want with me, I wonder?"

"Just the pure pleasure of your company, my dear; that is all I crave."

Her cheeks flooded with colour. "You are too kind to me."

"Tush. My needs are quite simple. I just wish to admire you as often as I can contrive."

She gave him a bold look. "I cannot imagine why, Sir Courteney."

He smiled. "Ah, you must understand your own charms. I am jaded, my dear. I have seen so much and I admit I have enjoyed my life, but nothing seems new to me — not until I met you, of course. You, Lady Astbury, are like constant springtime to me, both fresh and beguiling."

"How kind of you to say so, Sir Courteney," she answered, feeling slightly embarrassed at such fulsome praise.

It was not as if she were a society beauty, used to such flummery.

He took out his snuff box and inhaled a pinch. "Do you not, Lady Astbury, grow weary of rusticating?" he asked as he put the box away again.

"Not at all," she answered, sighing contentedly. "I find country life agrees with me. However," she added, with a chuckle, "when I arrived here and saw the place, I declare I thought it would be the end of me."

"Happily that was not so. However, I am bound to admit at Hartington Priory we often grow weary. There is a lack of diversions in the country and we needs must make our own."

"Which are often more enjoyable."

"Exactly," he said with satisfaction. "I am so glad we are in agreement." He licked his lips before venturing, "There is a deal of history attached to the Priory which would be of interest to you, I fancy, my lady."

"Oh, indeed. Family histories fascinate me and I know Hartington Priory has a great many associations."

"It is a great source of pride to me," he admitted, "and occasionally, when there are enough of us we find it diverting to stage . . . an historical pageant in the old Priory. Mayhap you would care to join us in our games on some future occasion."

He looked at her speculatively and for some reason Elyssa was more than a little discomforted. Hesitantly she replied, "I shall certainly mention it to Lord Astbury."

Sir Courteney frowned. "By all means, but in all honesty I must say that I do not believe his lordship would enjoy our diversions. From past knowledge I recall Lord Astbury and I rarely enjoyed similar pursuits."

Elyssa smiled brightly. "In that event, Sir Courteney, I doubt if I should either."

A clock somewhere chimed the hour and she got to her feet, causing him to do so, too.

"It has been such a pleasure seeing you but I must return indoors now. There are matters which necessitate my attention. Be pleased to excuse me."

He pressed his lips to her hand. "Regretfully, Lady Astbury, I take my farewell, and I only hope you may change your mind and enjoy my hospitality at Hartington Priory before too long a time has passed. You may be certain to receive an invitation."

She smiled again, withdrawing her hand as soon as possible. "Good day to you, Sir Courteney."

"Until we meet again," he murmured, and as she hurried away with Tinker running at her heels, Elyssa was aware of his eyes following her until she was out of sight.

* * *

"Be pleased to sit down, Elyssa."

She walked the length of the library — fortunately the earl was perusing some papers so she was not obliged to suffer his scrutiny — and sat down in a chair in front of the desk.

Beyond the library window was the pastoral scene of fields, trees and hedgerows which she found so soothing, but the lengthy silence soon began to wear on her nerves.

He looked up at last, putting down the papers he had been studying. "I take it that the lesson went well?" he asked in a conversational tone, exhibiting none of the anger of the previous night.

"As always. The children are exceeding keen. There is no obligation for them to come, and yet they do." She hesitated before adding, "I only hope you were not in any way inconvenienced by their presence."

"I saw nothing of them," he admitted, "but heard their chatter and laughter from afar as they left." He hesitated before saying a mite shamefacedly, "I wish to beg your pardon after last night, Elyssa. I behaved boorishly."

"You were bosky," she answered unequivocally.

"Yes, and although I still do not approve of what you are doing, there was no necessity for me to instigate such unpleasantness."

"It is of no import."

"You relieve me," he answered with feeling.

He sat down on the edge of the desk, gazing at her. "You are ahead of your time, Elyssa. One day I envisage all will read and write, even the humblest cottager."

"I hope so, and I am grateful you do not intend to end my endeavours."

"If it pleases you." He waved his hand in the air dismissively before asking, "Do you know what I have been about today?"

She looked startled. "I believe you have been with your land-steward discussing estate matters."

"That meeting has been adjourned until the morrow. Instead of what I planned, Allardice has been giving me a tour of my own house. In truth, Elyssa, I scarce recognized it."

She transferred her attention to her clenched hands. "I am sorry if what I have done has displeased you."

"What made you embark upon such an ambitious course?"

"When I arrived here there was scarcely a room habitable. I could not believe the scale of the neglect. It was impossible for anyone to live here with the least degree of comfort." She looked up at him but for once he could not hold her firm gaze. "I began by making one or two rooms more comfortable for my own use and then for some reason continued. I tried not to invite too much expense."

"You have done very well."

She looked up sharply, hardly daring to believe her ears. "Does that mean you are not, after all, angry?"

He shrugged slightly. "I confess I was at first angered by your presumption but I have come to realize the house is a wife's preserve and as such she mut have her head. And I admit the changes were necessary."

"Oh, indeed they were. And I am heartily relieved you are not angry. I was persuaded everything I did must anger you."

He shifted uncomfortably at so

accurate an observation. "You mustn't mind my manner too much. I am merely unused to wedded life. A wife is something I had not expected to acquire that evening."

Elyssa returned her attention to her clasped hands. "You must think me a poor creature indeed for not uttering a protest."

"But as I recall you did, and as you know it was in vain. You had no choice in the matter. Protest to any greater degree would have been just as useless."

"I felt as distressed as you only it didn't seem to matter; I believed at that time I would die before long and you would not be obliged to tolerate me for more than a few months."

He almost flinched at the echoing of his own thoughts at that time. It pained him now to know she had been aware of them and accepted her assumed fate so stoically.

"Your health has improved amazingly," he said a moment later in a rallying voice. "I am glad to note it, Elyssa."

She looked up again, her green eyes disconcertingly frank. "Are you? Are you really?"

He was obliged to look away. "I assure you I am."

He went to stand by the window and stared out. Elyssa took the opportunity of studying his proud profile, the high-bridged nose, the dark eyes fringed with long lashes and a pair of wide lips which could express disapproval and delight, and a good deal more, she thought uncomfortably.

After a moment he said, "We have had time to become reconciled to our fate. Mayhap whilst I am here we can get to know one another a little better. It would make for better understanding."

"Our paths are bound to cross on occasions, I dare say," she murmured when he paused.

A moment later he moved away from the window. "I have spoken to the men working on the house and they assure me all the rooms will soon be completed."

She smiled weakly. "What shall I find to occupy me when they are?"

"I am persuaded you will contrive." After another pause he added, giving her a shrewd look, "No doubt you have matters pressing at this very moment, so I shall not detain you any longer."

He moved away from the desk and Elyssa got to her feet. Just as she was about to go she turned to him again. She waited there hopefully and becoming aware of her remaining presence he turned to look at her again with his customarily disinterested stare.

"Is there something more you wish to discuss with me?"

She bit her lip apprehensively before asking in a quick, breathless voice, "Could you possibly be kinder to my sister-in-law?"

A look of amazement crossed his face and she went on with some difficulty, "Sophia feels acutely that she is not wanted here and I would be obliged if you would endeavour to be more friendly towards her, for my sake if for nothing else."

A slow smile replaced the look of amazement. "Did she ask you to speak to me?"

Elyssa's eyes opened wide. "No! She would not humiliate herself to do so. But I do know she is embarrassed and feels, perhaps, an intruder. She is a guest here and I beseech you to treat her as such."

"The impudent baggage!" he cried and began to laugh.

Stung, Elyssa hurried from the library, feeling bemused at his laughter which still echoed in her ears long after she was out of earshot.

9

THE stableyard was muddy and Elyssa was obliged to hold up the skirt of her riding habit as she walked carefully across the cobbles. However, with Tinker running at her heels it was not so easy.

A stable door opened as she approached and one of the boys came out leading two saddled horses.

"Only Stardust is needed this morning, Arthur," Elyssa told him. "Mrs Fontwell will not be riding today."

Even as she spoke, she frowned, for her sister-in-law during the two weeks of her stay had frequently found excuses to remain in the house. She seemed not the least interested in seeing something of the countryside which she declared she had come to enjoy.

The stableboy helped her mount, handing her the riding whip once she was settled in the saddle.

"See that Tinker doesn't run off," she told the stableboy, who grinned.

"I'll see he gets fed, too, ma'am, never you fear."

His reward was a grateful smile. With a groom in attendance she guided her mount out of the yard and the moment they were beyond the house she gave her horse its head, luxuriating in the feel of the breeze on her cheeks. As it permeated her lungs she could almost feel it doing her good. Strength seemed to invade her entire being.

As on previous occasions she found herself riding in the direction of Sir Courteney Hartington's land, mainly because the baronet was often to be met whilst riding, too. Elyssa was not averse to his company on occasions as he diverted her mind and amused her.

However, he was still an enigma to her. He had extended the utmost charm and courtesy towards her and as it was for the first time in her life she was more than a little flattered, but nevertheless there was something about him which also alarmed her. It was something in the way he looked at her as no man had done before.

The problem was, Elyssa told herself, she was unused to the ways of men. None had ever looked upon her with the slightest admiration before. When thinking of such matters she invariably tried not to bring the earl to mind, for she was finding, of late, that thoughts of the man she had married were too disconcerting to examine at close quarters. The earl alarmed and disturbed her far more than any other man, even Sir Courteney Hartington. Up until his arrival she had despised him heartily, for accepting the vile wager, feeling he was a man of a similar stamp to her own father for whom she harboured no true affection, but now she was not so certain.

The earl, she was forced to concede, had shown a more agreeable side to his nature, even though she knew he must be railing against a fate which sent him so unsuitable a wife. Elyssa could smile at the thought. She could not pity him, for she regarded it as his just fate because he had played a game of chance for reckless stakes.

She supposed her own fate was to remain for the rest of her life at Chipping Park, something which did not daunt her. She had never enjoyed the social round — her debutante year had been a veritable nightmare with one after another of her acquaintances marrying, and her mother irritated because she, herself, did not invite more suitors.

No, the thought of staying here where she had known so much contentment and where there were little demands upon her emotions, could only please her, and yet now, for the first time in her life, she yearned for a greater fulfilment even though she was not certain how it could be achieved.

Elyssa eased her horse into a canter when she heard the thunder of hooves behind her. Turning in the saddle she was surprised to see, not Sir Courteney Hartington but Charles Lamont approaching at a gallop. He was riding one of his host's splendid horses and as he approached bestowed upon her one of his rare smiles. He reigned in his horse when he reached her and bowed low in the saddle.

"Good day to you, Lady Astbury."

"And to you, Mr Lamont," she answered, looking at him curiously.

"This is a most fortunate encounter, for I have only just called in at Chipping Park in the hope of seeing you."

"I am at your disposal now, Mr Lamont."

"'Twas not a matter of great import, I assure you. 'Twas merely that Sir Courteney wished to invite Lord Astbury, yourself and Mrs Fontwell to dinner at the Priory, and I undertook the pleasure of delivering the invitation myself."

"That was very kind of you."

He eyed her speculatively for a moment or two before asking, "May I ride a pace with you, Lady Astbury?"

Over the past few months Elyssa had come to enjoy the solicitude of her rides, but nevertheless said, "You may, of course, Mr Lamont."

As they rode on she said, mindful of previous occasions when he had been less than communicative, "I trust Mrs Lamont is in good health?"

"She always enjoys good health, my lady, and indeed we are both gratified to find you in such good spirits, too. Marriage, if I may venture to say so, ma'am, has been of the greatest benefit to you."

She smiled faintly. "There can be no doubt of it. Do you, speaking just between ourselves, of course, believe Lord Astbury has similarly benefited by way of marriage?"

The young man was obviously taken aback by such a question, but soon recovered himself to answer, "How can it fail to, ma'am?"

"My husband has so few relatives it is therefore fitting for you and Mrs

Lamont to be residing nearby. You are his heir, I understand."

"At this moment," the young man answered, sitting stiffly in the saddle. "Naturally his marriage has reduced somewhat those expectations."

"The unexpected often occurs," she mused. "I believe Astbury didn't expect to inherit the title either and would have been quite content to remain an officer of dragoons."

Charles Lamont's face grew pink beneath his face-powder. "I cannot think him such an addle-pate."

"I take it you would not be so reluctant."

His colour grew even deeper. "If Lord Astbury were unfortunate enough to leave no son I would deem it my duty to take on his responsibilities, ma'am."

"You possess a rare sense of duty, Mr Lamont. It is indeed admirable in you."

"Rustication is not one of his lordship's favourite pursuits," the young man said thoughtfully a moment later. "I would not expect him to stay at Chipping Park for much longer."

Elyssa smiled faintly. "I am not in his confidence in that respect, Mr Lamont. Certainly the estate has been badly neglected and there is a deal for him to do here, but I doubt if his stay will be overlong."

"Lord Astbury's predilection for the diversions of London are well known, but mayhap he will be content to rusticate whilst he has the company of two exquisite ladies. A wife who is all condescension and charm, and of course Mrs Fontwell."

Elyssa laughed. "Mrs Fontwell, as you must know, is my sister-in-law and staying as my guest, however . . . "

He smiled as she spoke. "Naturally, ma'am. I would not venture to suggest anything else, I assure you, but let me say I have never admired a woman more her tolerance and dignity in what could well have been a delicate situation." She brought her horse to a standstill and stared at him as he went on, "There are some who might question the wisdom of such a . . . situation, but you are, may I say, a model for all which is civilized in our society?"

His smiling face mocked her. Elyssa was certain the memory of it would remain for ever in her mind. For a moment she had not understood what he was trying to say, but almost like a thunderbolt the truth of the situation became clear to her and she cursed herself silently for being such a fool.

The arrival of the earl close on the heels of Sophia was no matter of chance after all, and how idiotic to believe a man such as he could actually be indifferent to someone as alluring as her sister-in-law. No wonder Sophia was so often absent from her side and the earl so concerned for his estate business for the first time. She wondered at which part of the estate the pair conducted their affair, or perhaps it was at the house all the time and only she had remained ignorant of it.

Not that she did not know he had mistresses, and she certainly did not care that he had, but the fact that this one was her own brother's wife and he had brought her to the country with him meant that they sought only to mock and humiliate her.

Tears of self-pity stung her eyes and she fought them back so her companion should not know of them.

Apparently unaware of the turmoil in her mind he looked up at the sky. "The storm clouds appear to be gathering, my lady. You must allow me to escort you back to Chipping Park."

Elyssa contrived to smile at him although the effort cost her dear. "Alas I cannot, Mr Lamont. I have a call to make before I can return, but pray do not feel the necessity to accompany me."

"Until we meet again, ma'am."

He bowed low in the saddle before

riding off. Elyssa watched him coldly for a few moments before turning her own horse and galloping furiously in the opposite direction. Her heart was full of hatred for the complacent Charles Lamont, and even more so for her husband and treacherous sister-in-law.

What a buffle-head they must think me, she reflected bitterly as the now freshening wind stung her cheeks and tore at her hat. How Sophia, who had never liked country life and who had not previously in the three years of her marriage to Desmond extended a hand of friendship towards Elyssa, must be laughing!

Elyssa did not draw in her reins until she had reached the tiny cottage on the edge of her husband's estate When the groom helped her to dismount she felt that a little of her anger had been spent, but she still did not know how she would face Sophia with any degree of equanimity in the future.

A gaggle of barefoot children came

rushing out of the cottage to greet her. They were poorly dressed but not quite as badly as they had been before Elyssa began to call. She spoke to all of them in turn and when their mother came out of the cottage, bobbing a curtsey, she indicated that the groom should hand over the basket he'd been carrying.

"Do be pleased to come inside, my lady," urged the farmer's wife breathless with excitement and wiping her workstained hands on her apron.

Elyssa did so, but for once was in no heart to speak with the children further. She looked around the one tiny room where the farmer, his wife and six children lived, slept and cooked. The fact constantly amazed her. Her own father had always bemoaned his poverty and yet they ate well, lived in a handsome house, had servants and were more than adequately clothed.

The farmer's wife set the basket on the table and couldn't resist an immediate peep inside. When she lifted the lid she gasped and her eyes grew bright.

"Ma'am, this is a feast!"

"It is only our leftovers, Mrs Jenkins. My husband is in residence at present and more food is prepared than is truly necessary. There is a good deal wasted. I'm so pleased it will be appreciated."

"That it is, ma'am. That it is." She looked at Elyssa again, her eyes shining. "The good Lord sent you to us, ma'am. I am convinced you are the answer to my prayers. After the terrible winter with no crops we couldn't have survived without your goodness." Elyssa turned away in embarrassment. "You must be truly blessed, ma'am."

Cursed, more like, she thought darkly.

"Will you sup with us, ma'am?"

Elyssa cast her a smile. "Not today, Mrs Jenkins. I have been out longer than I should."

She walked across to the cradle near the fire and gazed down at the sleeping baby. "Young Alice is thriving now, I am glad to see."

"Aye, she is, thanks to you, ma'am."

"It was one of my housekeeper's remedies which cured her of the ague," Elyssa said quickly. "I assure you it was nothing to do with me."

"But if you hadn't called in that day and found her so ill we'd never have had that stuff and our little Alice'd be dead now." She put one hand on her rounded stomach. "The next one'll be named for you, ma'am." She laughed self-consciously. "A fine name for a farmer's brat."

"It may just be a boy," Elyssa pointed out.

"Then it'll be named for 'is lordship if he doesn't object, that is."

"I don't see why he should. What you name your baby is none of his concern."

"Young Tom's been reading that book you gave him, ma'am. Read us a piece last night. Can't believe my Tom can actually read just like his betters."

"Tom's a good pupil, Mrs Jenkins. He's a very bright boy."

"Reads all the time when his pa doesn't want him to work. The trouble is, Mr Jenkins thinks it a waste of time him going up to the big house every week to learn his letters."

Elyssa drew a sigh. "It seems that men think similarly, Mrs Jenkins. Lord Astbury regards it as a waste of time, too, but I intend to continue as long as the children keep on coming."

The baby began to stir and Elyssa returned her attention to the cradle, kneeling down and wriggling her fingers in front of the child.

One pink hand clamped around her finger and Mrs Jenkins said, "Young Alice has yet to learn her place, ma'am."

The baby continued to cling on to Elyssa's finger even when she started with alarm at the sound of hoof beats approaching and the whinneying of her own horse outside.

Moments later the earl, accompanied

by his land steward, came striding into the cottage. He looked around and his eyes fixed themselves at last on Elyssa.

"What a charming picture you present, my dear," he said immediately with no great pleasure apparent in his manner.

At last she managed to extricate her finger from the baby's grip and struggled to her feet.

"You never cease to surprise me. Who would have thought I would encounter you today so far from the house? Or mayhap I should have known."

He glanced around again and Mrs Jenkins and her children sank fearfully into the corner which surprised Elyssa somewhat.

"Are you often to be found in farm labourers' cottages?" he asked, obviously irritated by her silence.

"Usually once a week," she answered at last, her heart full of hatred for him, "but I was just about to leave." She managed to smile at Mrs Jenkins. "I shall call again."

The woman bobbed a curtsey and Elyssa walked past her husband and out into the open again. Fed by her anger over Sophia she turned to him as he followed her.

"If you condescended to spend as much time improving your estate as you do to pleasurable pursuits I would not be obliged to dispense charity to these good people."

The groom handed her into the saddle and she immediately rode on at a fast pace. Moments later, however, he had caught up with her, dismissing the groom who'd been struggling to keep up with his mistress.

"Where are you going in such a hurry?" he asked, holding on to the horse's bridle so she could not gallop off again.

She refused to look at him. "I am returning to Chipping Park. Why have you dismissed my groom?"

"The poor fellow looked in need of a

rest from chasing after you, and I also wish to ride with you myself."

She cast him a quick, scornful look. "What a waste of your precious time! Have you no estate business to attend to?"

"More than I had thought, if you are to be believed."

She didn't reply and he went on, "I take it you have no objection to my riding back with you?"

"If I did it would make no odds."

He frowned. "I wonder what has put you out of countenance, Elyssa. 'Tis most unlike you."

"You can have no notion what I am really like but you are still constantly disapproving of me."

"You are mistaken. I admire you, but you must forgive me if you misconstrue my concern for you. Those cottagers are for ever falling foul of fevers and pestilence, and I only fear for your health."

"Is your concern for my health the reason why you sent me to the country to a damp and inhospitable house?" When he merely stared ahead she went on, "Those cottagers should be able to look after themselves, I agree, but they cannot so I do not intend to stand aside and see children starve or die of fever when such a course is easily avoided and at no great cost to you."

"As you wish, Elyssa," he answered coldly and urged his horse into a canter.

Elyssa had no option but to follow and hoped that this would signal the end of that particular conversation. A few minutes later when the rain began to come down he called to her to follow him to a half-ruined cottage by the path through the wood.

The rain was already falling heavily and he quickly tethered the horses whilst she hurried into the comparative dryness of the interior which, by the look of it, had been uninhabited for years. She walked immediately to the gap in the wall which had once served as a window, watching the rain slanting down. She hoped it would quickly cease and thus cut short her time alone with him.

A few moments later he followed her inside brushing the rain off his coat sleeves. After giving him a cursory glance Elyssa turned away again to continue gazing out of the window, aware that as well as rousing her to anger, his close proximity discomforted her in a different way she could not understand.

"This cottage is a fortunate find," he murmured and she was aware he was staring at her curiously.

"I have often sheltered here on similar days. I really believed no one else knew about it."

"I know of it only because I have passed it on several occasions on my way back to the house. I wonder what became of the tenants. I shall have to find out. I don't like empty cottages; they bring in no income and this place must have been unoccupied for some years."

Elyssa continued to look out of the window. "Rumour has it that the woodcutter who lived here had but one daughter. She died mysteriously and afterwards, when he could bear the loneliness and memories no longer, her father left." She glanced at him. "It is said she was at the Priory when it happened but I cannot conceive that is true."

He drew a small sigh. "Such fanciful tattle dies hard. Rumour feeds upon itself and becomes a veritable monster which nothing and no one can kill." After a moment's pause he stared at her hard and said abruptly, "Elyssa, I have the oddest feeling you resent my returning to Chipping Park."

"I didn't mean to let it show. It isn't true resentment, but you must understand that after I came here my life was pleasant and uncomplicated for the first time in my life."

"Do you consider my return a complication?" He sounded resentful which she considered odd as he had never liked her company either.

She shook her head. "No, not really. It's very difficult to explain my feelings, but more to the point it isn't important."

"Dammit, woman, will you look at me when I talk to you!"

Obediently she did turn and gazed at him unblinkingly. "Why do you always give the impression that you're a hard and unfeeling brute, Astbury?"

He looked taken aback. "Am I not, in truth?"

"Not as much as you would have everyone believe."

He smiled ironically. "I am as I appear, my dear. Did I not after all send you to the country in the hope that the damp would affect you adversely?"

"I don't blame you for that. Had I been able I would have done the same. If possible I would have consigned you to the Devil."

"And now?"

She couldn't trust herself to answer

162

and was forced to turn away once more even though she risked his wrath, but he was not content to allow her to escape. He caught her arm and pulled her round to face him. She fought her own feeling of anger, aware that his own dark eyes flashed with fire.

"Your presence means nothing to me, if you insist upon knowing," she said in a steady voice, "but I wish you had not asked Sophia to come here, too."

His eyes narrowed. "I? It was you who issued the invitation."

"It was contrived; her visit to coincide with yours."

He gripped her arm even more tightly. "What has she been saying to you?"

Elyssa smiled then. "Nothing, but our neighbours know well enough what is going on and I don't doubt the servants do, too. I am humiliated by the knowledge of what she really means to you."

He let her arm go at last, much to her relief. He nodded slowly. "At last I see. Our neighbours, eh? I am persuaded they would not resist the temptation to stir the stew, but I did not connive at this visit nor did I wish her to come here. It was her own doing."

"How fortunate for you!"

"Elyssa, I did not want her here."

She tossed her head back proudly. "Do not flatter yourself I care with whom or with what manner of female you associate. I merely object to my sister-in-law coming here in the pretence she wishes to visit me."

"I never considered her to be the sort of person who would bestow friendship upon another female," he told her sarcastically.

She took the opportunity of turning away again. "You may, of course, do as you please. I forget myself. She is welcome but I am here out of sufferance only."

"No, you are not that," he answered

in a surprisingly gentle voice. "Once perhaps, but no longer."

"There is no use pretending that a marriage, contracted in such a way, can lead to anything else but frustration and bitterness."

"Did you know that your father cheated that night?"

Elyssa stiffened and hesitated before saying, "Yes, but I was certain you did not."

"He must have thought me as cunning as a dead pig. He had the cards in the palm of his hand."

She shook her head in bewilderment. "If you knew, why in heaven's name did you not denounce him?"

It was the earl's turn to avert his face. "I once killed a man in a duel over cheating at cards. It afforded me no satisfaction and I had no wish to repeat the experience." When she cast him a curious glance he averted his eyes again. "That isn't strictly true, Elyssa. I wanted to win and I didn't care that Sir Rupert had cheated to enable me to do

165

so. You see, I believed his daughter to be . . . Sophia."

Elyssa sank back against the wall. "I see," she whispered. "What a bufflehead I am not to have realized it earlier."

"I am only telling you now because it is of no more consequence."

"Is it not?" she asked in a dull voice.

"Oh, Elyssa, you must know that a man's mistress is a thing apart from his wife."

"She is here."

"She is here because of *you*."

Stiffening, she retorted, "I have already told you I do not care."

"Good," he answered briskly, "because I have been thinking that when I return to Town you might like to accompany me."

Her eyes narrowed suspiciously. "Why?"

He shrugged his broad shoulders as he poked with the toe of his boot at a pile of rags in the corner. "You might wish to enjoy the diversions, shop in the Strand, meet old friends and exchange *on dits* over a dish of tea. Time has passed; the tattle will have been forgotten."

"If you believe that you are a fool, Astbury, and I do not deem you one," she answered, an unexpected edge of bitterness to her voice.

He frowned. "Do you care so much what is said of you?"

"That you actually won me in a wager? That you prefer my sister-in-law but was cheated into marrying me? That you hide me in the country like some mad relative? No, of course I do not mind so small a bagatelle! I am content to be here, away from gossiping females and bosky men."

"You cannot mean to rusticate for the rest of your life."

"Why not? You are free to do as you please in Town. This arrangement of ours can only please you."

He fixed her with a steely look. "But I wish you to take your place in Society, Elyssa. I insist upon it."

Her hands tightened on her riding crop. "You may wish me to take up my place in Society but do you also wish me to take my place in your bed?" She turned on her heel, her eyes flashing green fire. "Of course you do not. After all there is Sophia and a string of other doxies to fawn over you, I don't doubt, and may I add I am most grateful to them all!"

Her anger was echoed by his. "You are a most provoking creature. No wonder Sir Rupert was so anxious to be rid of you by any means possible."

Furious at his taunt, she lunged forward with her riding crop and he took the full force of it on his hand. Wresting it from her he pushed her back against the wall and then snapped the stick into two pieces, throwing them to the floor.

Elyssa cowered against the wall, her anger replaced now with a numbing fear. She knew him so little. It was entirely possible he could do her harm, so great was his fury and there was no one who could help her.

Her eyes were wide with fear as he caught hold of her once again. "Unhand me!" she cried in desperation although it was clear he would do no such thing.

"Not until you're made to be sorry for striking me."

"I cannot be repentant," she gasped. "It is you who is provoking and I hate you."

Although she tried desperately to free herself from his grip his strength with so little effort outstripped her own. But he did not beat her as she feared. Before she had a chance to realize his intention his lips pressed down on hers roughly, bruising her with their intensity. Elyssa struggled desperately to be free of his passionate embrace despite an unfamiliar emotion it aroused in her. Momentarily she capitulated gladly until, becoming aware of it, he drew away at last.

She stared at him in horror at her

own wantonness but when it seemed he would take her into his arms again she rushed past him, out into the rain. Heedless to the downpour now, she untethered her horse with trembling fingers, struggled to mount him, and when she managed to do so, galloped off at full speed towards the house.

10

THE earl and Sophia Fontwell faced each other across the mahogany dining table. She merely picked at the food set in front of her whilst she watched him consume a hearty meal with gusto.

"Elyssa has retired with a headache," she said at last to break the lengthy silence which was beginning to annoy her.

The earl, whose wine glass was halfway between the table and his lips looked at her at last. "So I believe."

"Her maid has given her laudanum, so she is like to be insensible 'til the morrow." When he made no reply she went on in a light, conversational tone, "She was always used to do this when someone put her out of countenance. As it is the first opportunity we have had to be alone together since our arrival I can only be grateful to whoever has caused her the vapours."

His eyes narrowed as he peered across the table. "What makes you think that anyone has?"

"The manner in which she returned to the house today, in great agitation and wet to the skin, followed not many minutes afterwards by you. 'Tis only a wonder she does not sicken and die."

The thought had evidently not occurred to him and he looked astounded. "Do you really think she might?"

Sophia laughed. "Elyssa will outlive us all, I fancy." She gave him a playful look then. "What did you do to cause such agitation in my poor sister-in-law?"

He looked away from her, returning his attention to the food once again. "If you really insist upon knowing, I kissed her."

His admission caused her to look at first astounded and then to laugh merrily. "La! 'Tis only a wonder she has not succumbed to a brain fever. Could you not have beaten her instead? I declare she would have preferred it."

The earl indicated that the table should be cleared. When the port arrived Sophia automatically began to get up.

He waved his hand in her direction. "Sit down. Sit down, Sophia. I have no mind for you to go just yet."

Her cheeks took on a flush of pleasure and she sank back into her seat as he dismissed the servants. "I had almost made up my mind that you were indifferent to me."

"A man would have to be made of stone for such sentiments."

"You have been avoiding me since you arrived."

"Stuff and nonsense. I have been exceeding busy. There is a deal of neglect to put to rights."

She sat back, looking happier now. "It is of no real matter, although I have been cast into the dismals for the past two weeks. It's so good of dear

Elyssa to allow us this time together. Tonight . . . ”

“Sophia, make no mistake, I am still displeased with you for coming here. I am not so easily placated.”

Her hands clenched on the table top. “Would you have me crawl at your feet for forgiveness?”

“Heaven forbid,” he replied, taking a sip of the port and savouring it appreciatively before filling the glass to the rim. “I just wish you to leave at the earliest possible moment.”

She drew back. “You jest.”

“My dear Sophia, do you never listen to what I say? Sufficient time has now elapsed for you to be able to take your leave of us with no further ado.”

“Elyssa does not care if I am here. Why do you make so much of it?”

He sighed and sat back in the chair, gazing at the port which glowed in a crystal glass in the candlelight.

“It appears that, unlike this port, our love does not travel well. What I enjoyed in Town I cannot truly appreciate here at Chipping Park and you do yourself a great injustice by staying."

Sophia digested the news for a moment or two before saying, "We are still what we are in Town. What you say does not make sense."

"It does to me."

"I wish I had not come. Had I thought you would not welcome me . . ."

"The fault lies with me, Sophia."

"Shall you call to see me when you return to Town?" she asked hesitantly.

"You have no fear."

He sipped at the wine as she got slowly to her feet, never taking her eyes from his face. "I have known you well enough to be able to tell when you're lying to me."

He laughed then. "Heed what you say, my dear, for I have called men out for less. Take heart you are a woman."

"A woman heartlessly abandoned by her lover."

"One of her lovers," he answered darkly.

"There is only *you*," she cried. "You cannot discard me so easily."

The earl was unperturbed by her histrionics and he eyed her languidly. "Why not indeed?"

"I will not allow you to discard me in this way."

"What will you do? Tell your husband? Oh, Sophia, there is nothing you can do. One cannot fan a flame which has died. I regret it as much as you do, you may be certain."

She walked slowly around the table, saying in an agitated way, "I cannot conceive what form of madness has afflicted you of late. When we return to Town your affection will be as great as it always was."

"Perchance you are correct." He reached for her hand and lifted it to his lips. "You are very lovely, Sophia. Whatever the future holds I shall never forget our happy hours together."

She snatched her hand away from

his and began to move towards the door. As he half rose from his seat she said, "You will certainly not forget, for whenever we meet you will be reminded of every minute you spent with me, but do not think you can come to me as you please, Astbury. Even if you grovel at my feet you will be repulsed." She cast him a look of disgust. "I cannot conceive that you discard me in favour of a vapid miss who cannot possibly make you happy for I am certain it is she who has caused this change in you."

"Sophia," he said in a warning tone, "do not think to go to Elyssa with this foolish tale."

"You need have no fear. She is welcome to you. She could not survive a twelvemonth of marriage to you, and you will be bored witless even before that!"

As the door closed behind her he sank down into the chair once again, sighing deeply. "Confounded females," he murmured, and then drew the decanter towards him, pouring a large measure of port into the glass.

* * *

When she heard a knock on her door Elyssa pushed her damp handkerchief under her pillow, sat up and pulled the shawl tight about her shoulders.

Her heart was beating fast and when Sophia's face peered round the door she didn't know whether to be glad or not. Her head sank back against the pillow in a gesture of languor. Undaunted Sophia came further into the room.

"I'm so glad to find you still awake."

"I was just about to go to sleep."

"How do you feel, Elyssa? I declare you do look a trifle hag-ridden, but are you in any way recovered?"

"No," came the unequivocal reply.

Nonetheless, Sophia came up to the bed, staring down at her sister-in-law, an expression of concern upon her face. "Astbury and I have been most concerned for your absence all evening."

Elyssa almost flinched at the coupling of their names, even though she had promised herself to be sophisticated and ignore the affair.

"I wonder that you noticed I was absent."

Sophia seated herself in a chair by the bed. "You seem sadly out of sorts, my dear. Is there anything I can do for you?"

"Only leave me alone, for I am not fit to entertain visitors at present."

Sophia toyed with the pearls which adorned her throat. "Astbury will be furious if he discovers I have spoken to you of this, but I am persuaded you know all about our relationship."

Elyssa looked at her wide-eyed. "Yours and mine, Sophia? Of course I do."

The other woman bit back a gasp of exasperation. "Astbury and me."

Elyssa looked away. "Oh, that. Of

course I do. I doubt if it is a secret in any quarter."

"You are amazing sophisticated, Elyssa, which I confess surprises me, but I am truly glad to see it in you. However," she mused, "there is one person who does not know and that is Desmond. He would be very angry to discover I have cuckolded him even though there are few enough married men who have not been at some time. He has not your degree of sophistication, I fear. You know how possessive and jealous he is. If he discovers what has been going on, Elyssa, he is like to call Astbury out. That would be most unpleasant for us all, I own."

"If Desmond were to run him through with his sabre you cannot imagine I would care. It would be the first brotherly act on my behalf that he had ever done."

Sophia looked irritated by Elyssa's nonchalant stance. "Astbury is more like to kill your brother."

At this truth Elyssa was forced to look away. "You need not fear, Sophia; do not think I would tell Desmond. My brother has never earned my loyalty, so he shall get none."

Almost indiscernibly Sophia sighed. "You are very wise, Elyssa."

"Wise, am I? Because I wish to avert the possibility of bloodshed? It has always been held that I am stupid and mayhap never more so than now."

"I have never thought so."

All signs of nonchalance were gone. Elyssa shot her a hateful look. "You must have done to think I would know nothing of your reason for being here."

Sophia smiled and looked at her sister-in-law askance. "One would almost believe you were jealous, but I cannot conceive that it is so. You could not be so old-fashioned, especially in view of the circumstances of your marriage."

"I jealous!" Elyssa cried. "How ludicrous a suggestion! You and Astbury may go to the devil for all I care. I am merely miffed that you purported to come here to see *me*."

Thoughtfully, Sophia replied, "We considered it best, but you need not worry unduly now, for I am to leave as soon as it can be arranged. No doubt Astbury will leave, too. Once again you will be alone here as you so obviously prefer."

She got to her feet, smiling down on a vexed Elyssa. "Good night, my dear. I trust that you will sleep well and awake feeling much more refreshed." She hesitated before adding, "Leave it to me to make certain no one disturbs you tonight, not even your husband."

As she sauntered towards the door, Elyssa's furious stare followed her every move. As the door closed behind her she pulled the covers up to her chin, hating everyone, especially herself for feeling so outraged about their relationship. She knew that even if their marriage had been contracted in the normal way she would have no right to feel such chagrin. Her own feelings perplexed her, as had the strange longing and anger which also afflicted her at frequent intervals.

Reluctantly she blew out the candle which stood on her bedside table and tried to rid her mind of thoughts of the earl kissing Sophia in much the same way he had kissed her that afternoon.

She was not to know that he was just finishing the bottle of port alone downstairs and Sophia, after succeeding in putting Elyssa out of countenance yet again, was sobbing bitterly in her maid's arms in the privacy of her own room.

11

ELYSSA discarded the samples of cloth she had been examining and drew a sigh. "I am so sorry, Mr Curtis, but I cannot decide which of these to order."

The man stared at her in some surprise and not a little disapproval, for the Countess of Astbury was sitting on the floor in the centre of the half-finished room with the cloth samples spread all around her. To a tradesman such as he it seemed she demeaned her high position. As she glanced again at one of the more favoured samples he thought that altogether she was not at all like the quality he usually served.

Lady Astbury always dressed neatly but with little flair, and she wore so little powder and only one patch.

"Mayhap the rose satin, my lady,"

he suggested. "After all you did favour that a while ago."

She shook her head as she looked at it doubtfully again. "I really am very sorry, Mr Curtis, but the decision must wait." She put a hand to her aching head. "My husband will be departing for London before long and I shall then have the time to give these matters the consideration they deserve."

She held out her hand to a footman who immediately came to help her to her feet. "Until that time," she added, "I really cannot think with any clarity."

She walked slowly to the uncurtained window, gazing out across the fields. She was certain the earl was somewhere out there with Sophia, for she had seen neither of them that morning. The thought of them being together constantly returned to torment her.

Whilst Mr Curtis gathered up his samples a footman came in and Elyssa looked at him expectantly.

"Sir Courteney Hartington and Mrs

Lamont are here, ma'am."

Elyssa felt like crying off meeting them, but acknowledged they would most probably divert her mind with their inconsequential chatter and as she left the room she said, "Have the tea kettle brought up. I shall be down in a few minutes."

Back in her room Dora helped her change into a more elaborate gown, tidied her hair and applied another patch to her cheek.

"'Tis no wonder Sir Courteney admires you so, ma'am."

Elyssa's cheeks grew pink. "I am persuaded it means little. He is merely being polite to a neighbour."

Dora gave her a wry look. "Don't you believe it, ma'am."

"I trust you are wrong, for I have no wish to acquire a gallant."

"Most ladies of quality have several."

"If that is so, Sir Courteney Hartington, charming as he most certainly is, would not be among mine. However, I shall continue to respond to him with politeness and no doubt he will keep on flirting with me."

"Oh, from all I have heard, Sir Courteney Hartington is not a man to be put off so easily, ma'am."

Elyssa looked at her with interest then. "Oh? What have you heard about him?"

Dora's cheeks grew more pink than they usually were. "That he's a rake, ma'am."

She began to tidy the dressing table and Elyssa asked, "Are not all men?"

"Yes, ma'am, I dare say they are."

"And what is said of Lord Astbury, Dora? Tell me that, if you please."

The girl continued to tidy the dressing table. "Very little, ma'am. After all, the servants here scarce know him yet."

Elyssa drew a small sigh but as she was about to leave the room she turned to her maid yet again. "Dora, which room does his lordship occupy?"

The maid was obviously taken aback

by such a question. "Room, ma'am?"

On hearing such prevarication her heart sank, fearing what she suspected was true. "Which bedchamber, Dora? The one adjoining this is yet to be completed."

The girl's face cleared. "The one that used to be called the Blue Room, ma'am, at the far end of the corridor."

It was Elyssa's turn to look surprised. "But only two rooms are complete; this one and that occupied by Mrs Fontwell."

"No, ma'am, that isn't true; at least not any longer. On the day after his arrival, his lordship spoke to the workmen and they managed to have that one fit enough to occupy by evening."

Elyssa was both relieved and amazed. "It seems my technique with these workmen is seriously in error, Dora, for they do not perform such miracles for me."

The maid looked relieved, too, so much so that Elyssa was bound to ask, "Dora, is there a deal of gossip about Mrs Fontwell going on amongst the servants?"

When Dora averted her eyes Elyssa had her answer and it was obvious the servants had known about it long before she had. She asked no more, not wishing to embarrass her maid whom she knew was devoted to her, but also because she had decided she did not wish to know more.

The footman in the hall flung open the drawing room doors and Elyssa walked in to greet her visitors who were awaiting her within.

Sir Courteney immediately came to kiss her hand. "What a vision of loveliness you are!" he declared and his look immediately embarrassed her.

"Indeed she is," Mrs Lamont agreed. She was dressed in a gown of dun coloured velvet with a matching cloak and feathered hat. She looked at Elyssa with interest before she smiled. "My dear, your appearance could well start a rage for rustication."

Elyssa smiled. "I believe many would benefit, Mrs Lamont."

The woman beamed. "Mrs Fontwell has been in high feather since she came here, too. Rarely have I seen anyone benefit from a stay in the country as she has done. Of course I am very happy to be here, too. Naturally, in addition to the benefit to my health it has been a pleasure to see my kinsfolk. Now that Astbury has such a charming wife I feel we may seek each other's company more often in the future."

She drew out a snuff box and took a pinch. At that moment the footman arrived bearing an enormous silver tray with tea kettle, caddy and delicate dishes of Rockingham china. The lackey lit the kettle with a taper before withdrawing and Elyssa seated herself at the table, unlocking the caddy with the key she carried in her pocket. She was glad of the diversion.

"I wonder if that blend is one of our very own," Mrs Lamont mused as she watched her.

Elyssa looked up in surprise. "I did not know you were engaged in the tea trade, Mrs Lamont."

"My late husband owned many ships which did the China run, although I have little connection any longer. Now we are related to an earl," she gave a deprecating little laugh, "and as my son is at present his heir, it would not be fitting to indulge in trade."

Whilst listening intently to what Mrs Lamont had to say Elyssa caught the eye of Sir Courteney who had been gazing at her admiringly, something which caused her to look away quickly.

When the tea brewed the lackey handed round the dishes. Mrs Lamont tasted hers before saying, "I do believe this is the very blend supped by the Emperor of China."

Sir Courteney languished on a sofa, one breeched leg crossing the other. His shoes bore diamond buckles, the buttons on his coat were gold. He was considered to be most elegant, but on reflection Elyssa found she preferred the rather less flamboyant and yet more elegant appearance of her own husband.

"I rode out today in the express hope of meeting you, my lady," he told her. "I was sorely disappointed."

"I was engaged in choosing furnishing materials for several of the rooms and had not the time."

"Sir Courteney," Mrs Lamont confided, "was afraid you would not join us for dinner tomorrow evening."

In truth Elyssa had forgotten all about the invitation after the trauma of the day before.

"I am a buffle-head indeed, Sir Courteney," she explained. "Such is the number of workmen present in the house and so many the occasion I am troubled for my opinion, I quite forgot my manners."

"Oh, my dear Lady Astbury, that is of no account. What is of the utmost import is if you can all come. I have some very special diversions planned. I am persuaded you will be vastly entertained by them."

Elyssa looked down at her cooling dish of tea. "My sister-in-law has intimated her intention of leaving Chipping Park in the near future. Mayhap she will have done so by the morrow."

"That is indeed a pity," he mused.

"Charles will be devastated," his mother lamented. "He is quite besotted by her, you know."

Elyssa smiled. "That is by no means uncommon, Mrs Lamont."

"Naturally, Lord Astbury will be here to escort you on the morrow," the woman ventured, casting a glance at Sir Courteney.

Elyssa hesitated to answer for a moment before smiling again and saying, "It is entirely possible that he will not be able to accept your hospitality. As you may know his visit here is like to be a short one and 'tis altogether possible that he, too, will be obliged to return to Town."

Sir Courteney sat up straight. "Much

as that grieves me, my lady, I sincerely beseech you to come in any event. There are many guests coming merely to make your acquaintance."

Her eyes opened wide. "That cannot be so, Sir Courteney."

"I assure you that it is."

Mrs Lamont's thin lips stretched into a smile. "'Tis no wonder, my dear. Foolish Sir Courteney oft sings your praises to all who will listen."

Elyssa's cheeks deepened in colour and the woman went on, "I do have to remind him that my relative has called a man out for less, and that he should be less impetuous when paying court to another man's wife."

Elyssa smiled faintly once again. "I can assure Sir Courteney that my husband would never call a man out on my account."

"If you were my wife," the baronet declared, "no man would be allowed to look upon you without incurring my wrath. Mayhap that is why Astbury has sent you here, to keep you from rash fellows who are most certain to fall in love with you."

Elyssa laughed. "You speak with a honeyed tongue but I thank you for your flummery. My husband removed me to the country for the sake of my health."

Mrs Lamont looked at her questioningly. "It has improved so much I dare say you will be contemplating a move back to Town."

"Not at present, Mrs Lamont," she replied, averting her eyes, and then, "More tea?"

"If you please; it is excellent," Mrs Lamont answered and then when it was served, "but do you intend to come to Hartington Priory on the morrow, my lady?"

It had been Elyssa's intention to refuse the invitation, for nothing was less attractive to her now than enduring Sir Courteney's adoration. It no longer flattered, merely irritated, and she wished only to be left alone. However, when she thought about the earl and

Sophia, her heart filled with anger and she had no intention of remaining isolated at Chipping Park for the rest of her life whilst he enjoyed every pleasure and diversion.

"Indeed I shall be there, Sir Courteney," she answered at last, bestowing upon him a smile. "You may rely upon it."

* * *

Just as the earl came striding into the hall Tinker came bounding up to him. He recoiled automatically but the mongrel merely began to wag his tail madly and then proceeded to lick the mud off his boots.

"What peculiar tastes you have," he murmured.

A moment later his attention was taken by a noise on the stairs and when he looked towards them it was to see Sophia standing on the upper landing, gazing down at him.

The dog growled deep in his throat

until the earl rebuked him sharply. Then Sophia came slowly down the stairs, watching him whilst a footman pulled off his muddy boots and replaced them with a pair of clean shoes.

When she reached the bottom of the stairs he got to his feet again, saying coolly, "Good afternoon, Sophia."

"The dog is not up to your usual exquisite taste, Astbury," she said with equal coolness although an ironic smile was playing about her lips.

"He is Elyssa's, not mine."

"He has taken quite a liking to you nevertheless. Really, you should take heed of what my sister-in-law is trying to say to you with that creature." He gave her a sharp look and she went on, tracing her finger along the top of a polished table. "She has a yearning for the helpless. You should give her a child; you would be doing her a kindness."

Irritably he answered, "I am in no mind to do a kindness to anyone."

Not at all put out she said, "I should

have remained upstairs, for you are plainly in a disagreeable mood today."

"If you insist upon remaining here against my wishes, you will witness a good deal more of my darker side," he answered wryly and then in a more conversational tone, "I note the carriage in the driveway and yet you are not in the drawing room with our visitors. 'Tis most unlike you, my dear."

"I do not find Sir Courteney as interesting as I had envisaged. Mayhap that is because he is only interested in green girls who know little of other men."

His face grew dark and a moment later he said ungraciously, "After our conversation the other evening I had thought you would be gone by now."

She eyed him maliciously. "Arrangements are in hand, but I did think you might also be making your way back to Town. I would not take an escort amiss. There are so many malcontents along the road to London. It is not safe to travel alone."

His glance was a mocking one. "You contrived to travel here in complete safety."

She gasped with exasperation. "You are the most ungallant man I have ever encountered."

He seemed not to take her strictures amiss and she went on heatedly, "Do not think I wish to stay longer, for I find the country decidedly boring. It will be a pleasure to return to Town where a score of men are importuning for my favours."

"I wish them all happy," he told her as he began to walk away.

"Do you not wish to pay your respects to Sir Courteney as your wife is doing with such alacrity?"

"No. Her effusions will suffice. You may deliver my regrets."

Sophia held her head higher. "If I do that, Astbury, your wife is bound to think we have been together."

He paused outside the library door to glance at her again with a newfound indifference. "I cannot help that. She

199

will believe it in any event and who shall blame her?"

He went into the library and closed the door with a decided snap before the footman could do so, leaving Sophia with a vexed expression on her face. She stood there for a few seconds before a smile crossed her face and then she went to the drawing room to deliver the earl's message. After all, she had his blessing to do so.

★ ★ ★

Elyssa missed nothing of her sister-in-law's glowing looks when she came into the drawing room.

"Oh, I beg you to accept my apologies for my absence," she said breathlessly, bestowing a smile upon them all.

"No doubt you were well-occupied elsewhere," Mrs Lamont ventured, casting Sophia a probing look.

"How understanding you are, Mrs Lamont. Lord Astbury begs me to ask you all to forgive him his absence. He charged me to explain only pressure of business keeps him away."

"How conscientious he is!" exclaimed Mrs Lamont.

Sophia smiled across the room at Elyssa who eyed her resentfully before saying, "There is no more tea left, I regret to say. Shall I send for some more water?"

"No, dearest, do not trouble on my account." She drew a deep sigh. "I am quite, *quite* replete, I assure you."

Chagrined, Elyssa was relieved to have her mind diverted a little by Mrs Lamont, but out of the corner of her eye she watched Sophia go to sit by Sir Courteney.

"Lady Astbury has imparted the devastating news that you are departing imminently," he ventured as she sat back in the seat.

"My sister-in-law is correct. There are matters in Town which demand my attention." He eyed her carefully and she went on, "I am, however, devastated at not being able to attend your rout on the morrow."

"I, too, regret that, Mrs Fontwell. I am persuaded you would have enjoyed my hospitality."

"Does my sister-in-law plan to go in any event?"

"She has indicated her intention of doing so, however," he hesitated, "it seems Lord Astbury finds rustics such as I undoubtedly must be, unworthy of patronage, unlike his worthy predecessor. I only hope he will not seek to discourage Lady Astbury from coming, for it seems a great pity; she enjoys so few diversions."

Sophia smiled into his eyes. "I think you need have no fear of Astbury's interference in his wife's enjoyment on this occasion. I have every reason to believe he will not be here."

Sir Courteney nodded his head slowly. "You do not surprise me overmuch, Mrs Fontwell. It is as I suspected."

Elyssa, from the other side of the

room, watched as the two laughed together and her heart was full of dark thoughts.

Mrs Lamont noted the direction of her eye and discerning something of what Elyssa was thinking at that moment, said, "Mrs Fontwell never fails to bewitch whichever gentleman she meets."

When there was no reply, Mrs Lamont cast her a curious look and then Elyssa said in quite a sharp tone, "What a pity we can have but one spouse!"

At this observation Mrs Lamont laughed gaily. "My dear, I am certain if that was at all possible, Astbury would not, could not, choose to have more than your own dear self." The woman got to her feet then and declared, "We shall detain you no longer."

Drawing an almost imperceptible sigh of relief Elyssa rose, too, eagerly bidding goodbye to her guests. She wished she could dismiss her unhappiness with as much ease.

12

"YOU shall now be rid of me," Sophia said defiantly as she stood in front of the earl's desk the following morning.

He gave her a disinterested look as he put down his copy of the *Evening Post*. Even though clad in a fur-lined travelling cape, she looked exquisitely beautiful. The sight of her once had been sufficient to melt any resolve, now it merely caused irritation.

"I am sorry your stay here has not been a happier one. I am persuaded you will be more content in London."

Her lip curled contemptuously. "What humbug, Astbury! You can have no notion what makes me content. Nor need you think I am fooled by your concern for your wife. You look upon her with as much contempt now as you did six months ago."

"Believe what you will, Sophia," he told her in a weary voice. "I am not much interested in your opinion."

"What I really mean to know is who has poisoned your mind against me? That beldam Kitty Lamont, no doubt. Oh, I know you and she were once lovers. Or is there someone else awaiting you in London? Horatia Dunnit, perchance, or Margaret Milsom?"

He drew a sigh. "This is a most undignified discussion, Sophia, and no good can possibly come of it. No doubt your horses grow restive, so you had best go with no further delay. Your anger does you no credit."

"Very well," she answered, drawing her head proudly, "but once you return to Town you will come back to me."

"If that proves to be so, I trust you will look upon me kindly."

"We shall see," she breathed before turning on her heel. When she reached the door she turned again and this time there was a smile upon her face. "Oh, by the by, a messenger arrived just as

I came downstairs and I undertook to deliver his missive to you."

He had already returned his attention to the newspaper but now he looked at her expectantly.

"Some fellow from Meltham, I think."

"I do have land there, but what on earth did he want?"

"He wanted you, Astbury. He was in no end of a pucker, too. It seems that the cattle at Meltham are afflicted by some pestilence which is killing them daily and the farmers don't know what to do about it."

The earl slapped the paper down on the desk, cursing roundly as he got to his feet. "I was at Meltham not a sen'night ago and all was perfectly in order."

"These things strike quickly," she said in a soft voice.

He nodded and seemed deep in thought. "This need not detain you, Sophia."

"Is there anything I can do?"

"Yes, ask a footman to send round for my horse and my land-steward. I shall have to go there myself. It sounds to be a serious business. The entire herd could be wiped out if something isn't done."

"Indeed," she murmured. "I shall also be taking my leave of Elyssa. Do you have any message for her?"

He was still deep in thought. "Yes, if you please. Explain the situation, if you will. I must be gone with no further delay and will not return 'til the morrow."

"I shall certainly inform her of that, Astbury." She blew him a kiss across the room. "Until we meet again in London."

She found Elyssa still in her room, going about her toilette.

"I am about to leave," she said without preamble, drawing on her gloves. "La! I shall be relieved to be able to shop in London and become acquainted with all the *on dits* once more. I declare I did not think to miss them all as much as I have."

Elyssa had been sitting at the dressing table but then got up to face her. "I am sorry you have found your stay so tiresome, Sophia."

The woman's face broke into an embarrassed smile. "Oh, I did not wish to convey a wrong impression, my dear. Rusticating has its advantages. My spirits are vastly improved, you may be sure."

"Then all that remains is for me to wish you a safe journey back home."

Sophia began to move back towards the door. "Entertain no fears on that score, my dear; with Astbury in attendance all the way, no doubt it will be as safe as can be."

Elyssa's eyes grew wide at the news although it was just as she had feared. "Do not tell me he is going too."

Sophia gave a little shrug. "Naturally."

"But he has not bid me goodbye."

"I was not aware of that. How shabby of him."

"Did he not send a message?" Elyssa

asked anxiously then.

"I am afraid not." She wrung her hands together. "Elyssa, my dear, I truly fear you love that rogue which distresses me greatly." Elyssa bit her lip and averted her eyes. It was not something she had so far admitted to herself. "How can you when he treats you so abominably? Even *I* do not love him."

Elyssa turned away. "Please, Sophia, you must go now before it grows too late. My feelings can mean nothing to you."

"But they do!" she answered artlessly. "It grieves me to see you wasting your affections, which I know can be deep and true, on one who is so indifferent to you."

"What would you have me do?" Elyssa asked in an expressionless voice. "I cannot change my husband as easily as I change my apron."

"What has one's husband to do with it?" came the scathing reply. "You must find your own gallant. Sir Courteney needs only the smallest encouragement to become your most faithful lover."

Still keeping her head averted, Elyssa answered, "I shall bear your advice in mind, Sophia."

"See that you do. I shall write to you, have no fear, and you must let me know all which transpires."

Elyssa watched her go, her heart heavy. A few minutes later, from a window in the long gallery, she watched Sophia's carriage depart with the earl on horse-back in front of it. The fact that they were not sharing the carriage gave her no comfort. She continued to watch until it was out of sight in the beech grove and then she couldn't see anyway for the tears which blinded her eyes. She laid her head against the cool glass, allowing the tears to flow at last.

For six months she had been alone and happy at Chipping Park. Now he and Sophia had gone it might be expected for life to return to normal again, but she knew that could never be. Her life was empty now, more so than it had ever been before, since he had unleashed a yearning in her which could not be stilled.

As she turned away at last, brushing the tears from her cheeks, she reflected sadly that although she loved him he was so besotted by Sophia he could not bear to be parted from her for even a day. There was no knowing when she would see him again and until she did there would be no true happiness to be had.

A footman came up to her unseen and she started nervously out of her thoughts. Her unhappiness made her snappish and she said, rather sharply, "What is it you want?"

"You ordered a carriage for this afternoon, ma'am . . . "

She had forgotten about Sir Courteney's invitation yet again. "Oh, yes . . . "

"What time do you wish to leave, ma'am?"

After a momentary hesitation she said in a firm voice, "Three-thirty I think will be soon enough."

He bowed and walked away. She still did not feel like attending the rout at Hartington Park, to laugh and to smile and be sociable, but pride would not allow her to remain at home alone to brood whilst Sophia and her husband revelled in each other's company at a posting inn on the road to London.

★ ★ ★

There were far more people present at the Priory than she had imagined. Somehow she had expected a small gathering of perhaps only herself, the Lamonts and Sir Courteney himself, but it seemed he was set to hold a full-scale rout.

When her presence was announced the host detached himself from a group of friends and came to greet her personally.

"My dear Lady Astbury, you are arrived at last; I feared you might cry off at the last moment and I was determined, in that event, to come along and bring you here myself."

She laughed uneasily, glancing around the room at all those unfamiliar faces. "How gallant of you, Sir Courteney!"

"Everyone is most anxious to make your acquaintance, my lady. Alas, I cannot keep your friendship for myself, although dare I hope I hold a special place in your heart?"

Returning her attention to him she answered, feeling a little uncomfortable, "Of course. You have always been so kind to me, and you are our closest neighbour."

"A fair word from you is payment enough." He paused before venturing, "'Tis apparent Lord Astbury and Mrs Fontwell are not coming."

Her cheeks heightened with colour at the reminder. "As I intimated yesterday, they have returned to Town."

"No doubt Mrs Fontwell will be well relieved to have the company of Lord Astbury on such shockingly unsafe roads. Now, my dear, I cannot delay your introduction any longer."

He escorted her to a group of gentlemen who sported fine wigs and clothes. Some swished fans to and fro and all had faces liberally adorned with powder and patch. All of them looked at her with great interest, much to her confusion, some of them through quizzing glasses.

The accumulation of their perfumes and pomades made her cough a little and she apologized shyly. It was the only reminder of the debilitating complaint from which she once suffered.

"Gad, Hartington," declared one of the group as he dropped his quizzing glass, "your praise was not, for once, empty."

"Does Sir Courteney often sing the praises of ladies of his acquaintance in so strong a voice?" Elyssa asked.

"Poultney, you are a cad," Sir Courteney cried petulantly. "Lady Astbury is a rare creature and I am uncommonly entranced by her."

The others laughed and Elyssa didn't

know whether to be embarrassed or pleased.

"To meet you, my lady, is well worth the day's journey from London," a macaroni told her and she looked surprised.

"Surely you cannot have come to Hartington Priory just to meet me?"

"And why not, my lady? You are worth a day's journey and more," another told her.

Her cheeks grew even more pink at such fulsome praise and Sir Courteney said, "You see, I do not exaggerate after all."

Elyssa was beginning to be discomforted and fanned herself furiously. "Sir Courteney, you cannot bring your friends to Hartington Park merely to introduce them to your acquaintances."

"They are gammoning you, my lady. Ignore their foolish funning, I beg of you."

Much to her relief, Mrs Lamont came along and rescued her. "Do not let those old rakes tease you, my dear."

"I cannot help but be pleased at their flattery, effusive as it is, and mayhap insincere."

"Oh, I am certain it is not that," she answered with a laugh. "You are quite uncommonly fetching."

"I'd as lief be commonly beautiful," she replied, pensive again as she thought of Astbury and Sophia.

"You are unused to such gatherings," Mrs Lamont went on. "You really have buried yourself away at Chipping Park for far too long. I cannot conceive what Astbury may be thinking of allowing it."

"It is what I wish, too, Mrs Lamont," she was quick to reply.

"Even so, I am quite persuaded you will enjoy this little diversion."

"I am already doing so," she answered, helping herself to a glass of champagne from one of the many trays being offered around. "But I confess I did not expect to see so many guests."

"Sir Courteney believes in entertaining

in style. Not for him the mundane."
She gulped back some champagne
before asking, "Where is that rascally
relative of mine? I had looked to see
him here this evening."

Much of Elyssa's pleasure evaporated
again at the reminder. "My husband
has been obliged to return to Town
— on urgent business," she added,
hastily gulping at the champagne which
immediately went to her head.

Charles Lamont came sauntering
up to them and as he passed a
footman bearing glasses of champagne
he grabbed one and handed it to her
with an elaborate flourish.

"You must not stand there with an
empty glass in your hand, Cousin
Elyssa," he told her and she did not
like the undue familiarity coming from
him.

"I believe I have had sufficient."

He laughed. "You are indeed a rare
creature but I refuse to accept that, for
the evening has not yet begun."

"I cannot conceive why anyone

should regard me as being out of the common."

He looked at her over his champagne glass. "My dear, if you were not, you would not be here tonight."

She frowned. "I do not quite understand your meaning, Mr Lamont."

"Charles is only funning," his mother answered, casting him a vexed look. "Drink has made him rash, I fear."

The announcement of dinner being served saved Elyssa the trouble of conversing further with the Lamonts. Not unexpectedly, Sir Courteney came to escort her into the dining room where a splendid feast was set out. All manner of meats, fowl and fish was put before them, but somehow Elyssa could not enjoy any of it.

Her mind was filled with the vision of the earl and Sophia together at that very same moment at some roadside inn, enjoying their dinner in the intimacy of a private parlour.

"My dear Lady Astbury, does not the food tempt you?"

It was her host's voice at her side which brought her mind back to where she really was and she knew then it had been a mistake to come.

"The food is exceptional, but I confess I am but a poor eater."

"You cannot be poor at anything you do."

She couldn't understand why she was so downhearted. The circumstance of their marriage in itself was sufficient to blight their lives for ever, so she had never had any expectation of happiness. Those six months alone as mistress of Chipping Park had lulled her into a false sense of security. If only, she thought, he had not come; in two short weeks all had been utterly changed and her newfound serenity shattered.

She glanced around the long mahogany table, lit at intervals by silver candelabra. The food was excellently cooked, the china and plate of the finest, and yet as she looked at the guests she felt they were not of the *haut ton* despite their fine clothes of damask and brocade, the glittering jewels worn by both gentlemen and ladies.

All, it seemed, drank too much, laughed too loudly and it appeared to Elyssa that there was far too much familiarity between the sexes for true gentility. Mild flirtation was both expected and accepted, but from what she was beginning to observe their behaviour went beyond what was proper in company. It was true that no one had yet behaved improperly to her, and yet just viewing it served to discompose her.

Mrs Lamont smiled at her son who was seated at her side. Charles at that moment, however, was looking down the table at Elyssa and said after a few moments, "Do you think that our relative is enjoying her evening, Mamma?"

"How can she fail?"

"She looks exceeding Friday-faced to me."

"The evening is not yet begun. She is not used to large gatherings, but she

220

will soon be more at ease."

"I cannot help but feel Astbury would be furious if he knew she was even here."

"Tush. He may not wish to be here himself but he does not care if she lives or dies, I can assure you."

"You cannot be sure about that, Mamma. Astbury is a devilishly deep fellow."

Mrs Lamont smiled faintly. "You forget that I have known him all his life — very well as a boy — and you may be sure he cares not a jot for this chit. The fact that she was won in a crooked game of cards could only serve to fuel his distaste of her. He will never forget that."

"Perchance he does not know Sir Rupert cheats when it suits him to do so?"

"My kinsman is usually up to snuff in all matters. He must suspect at the very least. Only think, he brought his paramour down to Chipping Park when he intended to stay only for two weeks.

Did not Mrs Fontwell confide in you herself stories of his devotion?"

"Yes, but . . . " he began doubtfully. "Men do not beget heirs by their mistresses."

"I have it on very good authority that they live quite separately. Even if that were not so, Lady Astbury's health would forebear her to carry a child successfully."

He cast her a sceptical look whilst picking at his boiled pigeon. "She is in the rudest health, Mamma. Can you not see that quite plainly?"

"Sir Courteney," she went on in a frosty tone, "tipped one of Astbury's servants a vail of several guineas for the information that their bedchambers are at opposite ends of a corridor. Do you suppose having brought Sophia Fontwell with him he would spend his nights with his wife?"

"Sir Courteney finds her fetching."

"He always prizes innocence above beauty, which we may be thankful Astbury never did. After this night

Hartington will not be much interested in her either any more. Besides," she added with a chuckle, "after the culmination of this evening's events she would kill him rather than allow him or any man within a room's length of her. Astbury, I feel, would abandon her entirely as a wanton woman and be glad to do so."

Charles Lamont chewed his food thoughtfully. "You contrived this, did you not?"

Mrs Lamont put down a chicken bone she had been chewing. "I merely put Hartington in mind of her, that is all. After he had made her acquaintance he could not resist the temptation and there was nothing more for me to do save to wait for an opportunity — and a full moon, of course."

"You are a scheming woman, Mamma," he said admiringly as she wiped her greasy fingers on a napkin.

She cast him a sideways glance. "Was it not you who said you were desperate to remain Astbury's heir to the title? You shall have it if you are patient. This marriage will not produce any hazards."

"I confess at first I wondered why you encouraged Sir Courteney to pay court to her. Now all is evident."

A selection of jellies, blancmanges and puddings were put on the table and, happier now, Charles Lamont helped himself to some of them, savouring every mouthful.

13

THE evening seemed to be wearing on interminably and it appeared to Elyssa that everyone was becoming more drunk. She sat on a sofa in the drawing room, watching those who were dancing although none of them were steady enough to keep strictly to the sets. Every so often laughter erupted from amongst the dancers much to the amusement of those who watched.

"Will you do me the honour of standing up with me for the next set?" Sir Courteney asked and she looked up at him.

"The hour grows exceeding late, Sir Courteney, and I feel I must soon be taking my leave."

He sat down at her side, looking concerned. "Oh, surely not. The evening has scarce begun."

"It has been most congenial, I confess, but I do feel a slight weariness."

He looked immediately concerned. "I am in total agreement that you should not overtax yourself."

"Your concern is so kind. Would you be pleased to order my carriage?"

He hesitated for a moment before smiling. "If it is your wish, my lady, but whilst it is being brought round will you not join me in one last drink?"

Elyssa laughed. "I am persuaded I have drunk far too much already. My head feels quite giddy."

"As one who has observed you closely, my lady, I take leave to doubt that is so." He got to his feet. "However, if you permit I shall send for your carriage to be brought round."

When he had gone she drew a sigh of relief. He returned not many minutes later with a glass of champagne in each hand.

"I have given the order, but before you go you must drink with me."

He handed her the glass which she took reluctantly. He held up his own, a faint smile on his rouged lips.

"Now, my lady, let us drink one last toast to close neighbours."

Obligingly she held up her glass, too, and although he made no attempt to drink his champagne he watched her carefully as she downed most of hers.

"You are a corrupting influence on me," she complained, laughing lightly.

Her head swam dangerously as he answered, glancing around at those within earshot, "What a delightful compliment."

"And now, alas, I must take my leave of you."

As she got to her feet her head swam again. She swayed and reached for the back of the sofa to steady herself, but Sir Courteney caught hold of her instead.

"My lady, I fear 'tis true you have drunk too much. You must be seated for a while until the faintness passes."

"No, no," she said quickly, putting

one hand to her reeling head. "I beg you not to trouble yourself. If you will but escort me to my carriage," she gasped as the room swayed before her eyes.

All around her many of the guests were eyeing her with amusement, most of them the worse for drink themselves, although Elyssa couldn't recall drinking more than she usually did.

"Perchance you should stay a little longer. It would be inadvisable for you to go in your present state."

"No. I must go home," she insisted. Chipping Park seemed to be a haven to her at that moment, but even as she spoke she discovered that her legs refused to move. "Sir Courteney . . ." she gasped in alarm.

She looked up at him and his face swam before her. There was a faint smile playing about his lips and his eyes seemed to be glittering with excitement. Just then, in her confused state, he looked positively evil and she tried to draw away from him even though she knew she was likely to fall. She tried to say something more but she could only sit down heavily on the sofa once again.

"Close your eyes, my lady," she heard him say in a soft coaxing voice. "Close your eyes for a moment and you will soon feel the better for it."

His advice seemed eminently sensible and yet she fought to keep her eyes open. It was a battle she could not possibly win.

The room grew dark although all the candles were still lit. She felt a great heaviness afflicting her eyelids and even though she continued to fight to keep them open they would not and after a while she laid her head back and allowed the darkness to enfold her.

★ ★ ★

The earl galloped his horse up the beech drive, fury tearing at his heart in much the same way as the wind pulled at his broadcloth surtout.

229

He jumped from the saddle almost before the horse had finally come to a standstill, handed the reins to a footman who had come hurrying out of the house at the sound of his approach and ran up the steps, taking two at a time, into the hall.

The house steward came forward, looking a mite surprised and somewhat ill at ease. "My lord, we did not expect you back so soon. Is something amiss?"

"Indeed it is. There is no cattle pestilence at Meltham. It was a hoax and I intend to know who has perpetrated it."

"Meltham, my lord? We understood you to be gone to London."

He divested the earl of his surtout and when he had done so his master turned abruptly on his heel to look at him accusingly. "*London*, by Jove! Who said so?"

"Her ladyship, my lord."

The earl frowned. "There is something exceeding odd going on and I intend to discover what it is. Do you know who the messenger was who came this morning with the news?"

"I know nothing about that, my lord."

Irritably, the earl cried, "Then find out who does! Who was on duty here when Mrs Fontwell was preparing to leave this morning?"

"It was I, my lord."

"Then you must have seen the messenger who came from Meltham."

"No, my lord. There was no messenger, I assure you, from Meltham or anywhere else."

The earl's eyes narrowed again. "The unprincipled jade! I see the way of it now. She will be heartily sorry for this." He looked at the house steward once more. "Where is Lady Astbury? Has she retired yet?"

"No, my lord. Her ladyship has not returned as yet."

"At this time! Where in heaven's name has she gone?"

"I believe she went to Hartington

231

Priory, my lord."

He glanced at the long case clock in the corner. "When did she go?"

"Her carriage was ordered for three-thirty, my lord."

"She has been gone an unconscionable time. Surely you must have expected her to return before this?"

"They keep late hours at Hartington Priory, I understand," the servant told him helpfully.

However, the earl was not much comforted by the news as he replied grimly, "So I believe."

"Hartington Priory is not so far, my lord, and the road between in fair condition. I don't think there can have been a mishap; there is a full moon tonight to light their way."

"Yes, so there is," his master mused and then, turning to the servant again, "Have a fresh horse saddled immediately. I shall ride over there and fetch her myself."

The house steward looked as if he were about to say something but thought better of it.

He bowed stiffly. "Yes, my lord."

The earl reached for his surtout, saying at the same time, "And make haste. I feel there is no time to lose."

* * *

Elyssa was aware of feeling cold. Her eyelids were heavy and she soon realized she was having a most peculiar dream. Her ears were filled with the sound of chanting. She tried hard to understand what the chanting was about.

"Surrender. Surrender unto Satan. All hail the Prince of Darkness."

With extreme difficulty she forced open her eyes at last. She didn't like the dream and wanted to be awake, but when her eyes at last managed to focus she was not after all looking up at the familiar tapestry tester, but at the vaulted ceiling of what seemed to be a church. Candles flickered in a constant draught and the chanting grew steadily louder.

"We surrender to you, Your Satanic Majesty."

It was no dream! Elyssa realized she was lying on an altar, clad not in her gown of blue lustrine but a white cambric gown which felt rough on her skin.

Her eyes opened wide with alarm then. Around her in the candlelight paced a score of people, all of them dressed in monks' robes or nuns' habits. Elyssa's throat was constricted with fear as she watched their pacing grow more quickly to match the chanting, and she was unable to move. She grew more alarmed when she realized that her hands and feet were tied. When she tugged at the bonds in desperation they seemed to hold her more fast.

Suddenly the chanting stopped. One of the nuns handed a monk a live cockerel and as she did so Elyssa was horrified to see it was Kitty Lamont in the travesty of a nun. When the monk stepped forward with the cockerel she could see his face quite clearly in the candlelight; it was Sir Courteney Hartington. It was then that her mind cleared a little. The drink, the drunken guests, their interest in her; she knew then it was no dream. Sir Courteney Hartington had planned to keep her here and for this vile purpose.

He seemed to tower over her, his eyes glittering with a crazed look she had seen only in her last moments before falling foul of the drugged champagne. He was a forbidding figure in the monk's cowl and she would have shrunk away from him if only the rope did not bind her so tightly.

"Oh, Lord of Darkness," he intoned. "Oh, Deliverer of all that is evil, purveyor of true power in the world, I dedicate this creature to your immortal greatness."

From the folds of the robe he brought out a knife, the blade of which gleamed wickedly in the candlelight. Elyssa's eyes opened wide with horror and fear as he brandished both the knife and the cockerel over her.

Then, with a flourish, he plunged the knife into the cockerel and she almost fainted with relief until the others began to chant again. Blood from the dead cockerel splattered on to the pristine whiteness of the gown. Revolted, Elyssa wanted to cry out but somehow she could not.

Sir Courteney put the bloodstained knife down on the altar and instead took up a cross which he held upside down in front of her.

"Oh, Lord of Darkness I am thine own representative on earth, and as such I claim this maiden in your name."

The others began to chant, "Aye, aye," and pace around the altar whilst Sir Courteney came towards Elyssa and climbed the few steps to where she was lying. His eyes were those of a madman; they all seemed mad.

"I claim you in the name of the Prince of Darkness!" he cried triumphantly to more excited cries from the others.

Elyssa tried to shrink away but even if the ropes had not tied her hands and feet, she was certain the after-effects of that drink were still with her and she would not have been able to escape him.

Suddenly as he loomed over her a figure detached itself from the others and cried, "No, you don't, Hartington!"

The chanting stopped. There was a groan of amazement and Elyssa didn't know whether her confused mind was playing tricks when she saw the earl step forward and draw his sword.

"Hold still, Hartington, or I'll run you through. I may do so in any event. Now," he told one of the acolytes nearest to him, "untie her and be quick about it."

As the man hastened to do the earl's bidding, Sir Courteney cried, "No! You cannot defy the will of Satan."

He was so maddened at the spoiling of his sport he snatched up the knife

237

from the altar and lunged forward with it.

A scream had been straining to escape Elyssa's throat and at the sight of Sir Courteney attacking the earl it did burst forth, echoing around the ancient walls of the ruined priory. Then almost as soon as it faded away she lapsed into welcome insensibility once more.

* * *

The chanting still echoed in her ears. Elyssa cried out to protest that what they did was wicked and as she did so her eyes opened again. There were no monks or nuns, just the familiar tapestry tester.

Relief caused her to moan out loud. A chair scraped on the floor and she turned her head almost fearfully to see a stranger getting to his feet at the bedside. She flinched away from him.

"Have no fear, my lady," he said. "All is now well."

238

"Oh, the Lord be praised," cried Dora's familiar voice.

Dora, Elyssa thought. If Dora is here I must be safe.

"Elyssa . . ."

She looked to the other side of the bed as the earl came into her line of vision, alive and apparently unhurt.

Tears of thankfulness began to well up in her eyes and he sat down on the counterpane, gathering her into his arms as she began to cry on his shoulder. Dora and the stranger withdrew and a moment later she heard the door click shut behind them.

"You're safe now," the earl told her. his voice no more than a whisper. "No one is going to hurt you ever again."

"Who . . . who is that man?" she stammered.

"He is only the local physician who assures me you are none the worse for your escapade."

At the reminder of her ordeal she trembled and his arms tightened about her.

"I was so afraid and then when you came it was like a miracle, but I thought he was going to kill you."

He laughed softly. "A coxcombe such as he! Elyssa, he has not the ability."

She drew away a little, gulping back her tears. "You . . . didn't . . . *kill* him, did you?"

"I would have done so, believe me, but some of his cronies held me back whilst another relieved him of that knife. I was rather sorry."

She sank back on to the pillows. "Sorry? I can only thank Providence that you did not."

"Such concern for that coxcombe," he mocked.

"For *you*, only for you. I would not have you spill blood on my behalf, even his."

"You are exceeding generous."

She put her hand up to her forehead. "Oh, my head! It aches so."

"Dr Humbert tells me it is due only to the vile nostrum they gave you. It

240

will soon be better after you've slept."

"I feel as if I've slept for an eternity already. I don't want to sleep any more."

"Nevertheless you will."

She frowned then, feeling confused. "You were there — with them. You were taking part in what they were doing! Do you often join in their ceremonies?"

He looked outraged. "You are quite wrong; I concealed myself amongst them only to await an opportune moment to free you."

"But you were gone to London with Sophia."

"I was gone to Meltham only because of her mischief making. No doubt she hoped my departure would cause our further estrangement. I trust that is what she had in mind, for if I discover she knew what Sir Courteney planned and deliberately enticed me away for him, she will most certainly be very sorry for it."

"You didn't go with Sophia," Elyssa

241

repeated in amazement.

"I had every intention of remaining here with you, which has become much more to my taste of late."

Her eyes grew misty and he went on, taking her hand into his, "The Season in London has all but ended, and in any event its attractions have faded for me. I just wish to spend the summer here with you."

"With me," she echoed, still amazed.

"What I told you was the truth; I had no notion she would be here, nor did I want her to be. She is nothing to me now."

Elyssa's heart lightened. "She fought for your interest which is more than I was capable of doing."

He raised her captive hand to his lips. "You, my sweet, captured my heart by being your own good self, and I entreat you never to change."

Her eyes grew brighter. "Do you truly . . . love me?"

"With all my heart."

She sat up again and put her arms

around him. "This is something I never dreamed might happen. My own love seemed so hopeless."

"I shall make up to you the humiliations of the past," he promised.

"It is of no matter now." She drew away then. "How *did* you find me?"

He kept hold of her hand, gently stroking it with his fingers. "When I returned to find you not yet home I rode over to Hartington Priory to fetch you myself. A servant there told me you had gone and the house was quiet. There was certainly no way you could have returned without passing me and, of course, I had heard talk of the diversions Sir Courteney provided for his guests so I rode back towards the ruined priory. Sure enough I saw the lights through the trees. I tethered my horse and approached on foot. Despite the rumours I could scarce believe what I saw through one of the windows. I was sorry then that I had come on my own, for I had no notion whether they were violent or not. However, I had no time to return for help and I did find it easy to get in without being seen. Most of them were foxed beyond reason."

"I might have been participating quite willingly," she teased.

"If I had thought so I would have left you there to go, quite literally, to the Devil, as Hartington styles himself."

Her eyes grew darker. "Why would anyone worship the Devil, Myles?"

"They do nothing of the kind. 'Tis only their vile notion of enjoyment. Not for them the tame ritual of drawing room or boudoir."

"That poor girl from the woodcutter's cottage; I can believe the rumours now."

He sighed. "Possibly she was given too much of whatever they gave you. We shall never know but one thing I am certain about, it will not happen again, I vow." He looked momentarily grim. "I only wish I could have arrived earlier to save you from that horrible ordeal. I shall never forgive your sister-in-law for that."

"Sophia no longer troubles me. She was ever foolish, but your relative, Kitty Lamont, was there, too."

"Do I not know?" he answered grimly. "Her rascally son, too. They will not show their faces in this county again, I vow."

"He is still your heir."

"Ah," he said, giving her a mischievous look, "but for how long?"

She managed to return a smile although she still looked troubled. "But what of Sir Courteney? The same cannot be said of him. He remains our nearest neighbour and like to be in the area from time to time whether we like the notion or not. How can I ever face him again?"

"You can be assured he will remain strictly to his side of the boundary in the future. As far as his revels are concerned, I have informed him in no uncertain terms that if I hear of such ceremonies being held again at the Priory I shall have him arrested for abduction."

"Oh, he is a truly corrupt man," she sighed. "I am only ashamed I never saw it in him earlier."

He smiled. "I am persuaded you once held a poor opinion of me."

She shook her head. "I could not have given my heart to anyone as wicked as that. I never considered you to be a wicked man."

She shuddered and he gathered her into his arms again, fiercely protective. After a moment his lips brushed her cheek and she drew away to look at him. Then his lips touched her lips, gently at first but in the wake of her own response with more passion. She met his kisses with a ferocious abandon which matched his own. At last, however, he laid her back against the pillows.

"This is madness."

"No, it is wonderful," she sighed, reaching up to touch his face.

"You really must rest."

"I know," she sighed again. "I do feel tired, but it is just when I am happiest, when I wish to get up and dance with joy that I feel so weary. It is very tiresome."

"'Tis no more than the physician envisaged, but there will be time enough for celebration when you're rested."

Despite the inevitable, she attempted valiantly to fight the weariness which threatened to overcome her and as her eyelids grew heavier she asked, "Will you stay by me?"

"Where else would I be?" he responded, moving from the counterpane to a chair at the bedside. Still retaining his grip on her hand he added, "Sleep well and tomorrow our life together will begin at last."

THE END

WITH SOMEBODY ELSE
Theresa Charles

Rosamond sets off for Cornwall with Hugo to meet his family, blissfully unaware of the shocks in store for her.

A SUMMER FOR STRANGERS
Claire Hamilton

Because she had lost her job, her flat and she had no money, Tabitha agreed to pose as Adam's future wife although she believed the scheme to be deceitful and cruel.

VILLA OF SINGING WATER
Angela Petron

The disquieting incidents that occurred at the Vatican and the Colosseum did not trouble Jan at first, but then they became increasingly unpleasant and alarming.

DOCTOR NAPIER'S NURSE
Pauline Ash

When cousins Midge and Derry are entered as probationer nurses on the same day but at different hospitals they agree to exchange identities.

A GIRL LIKE JULIE
Louise Ellis

Caroline absolutely adored Hugh Barrington, but then Julie Crane came into their lives. Julie was the kind of girl who attracts men without even trying.

COUNTRY DOCTOR
Paula Lindsay

When Evan Richmond bought a practice in a remote country village he did not realise that a casual encounter would lead to the loss of his heart.